My LONDON
the Great Cesspool

EAST: 111C BUTCHER STREET, EC

WEST: 221B BAKER STREET, W

1) THE DIOGENES CLUB

2) CAFÉ ROYAL

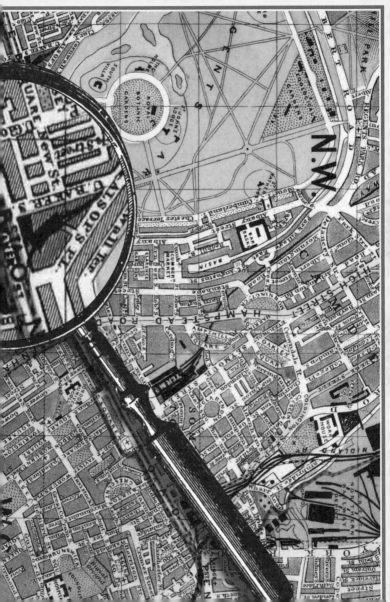

MORIARTY

A random collection
of Prof. James
Moriarty's
workings brought
together by
Col. Sebastian
Moran

Published in 2011 by New Holland Publishers (UK) Ltd
London • Cape Town • Sydney • Auckland
www.newhollandpublishers.com
Garfield House, 86–88 Edgware Road, London W2 2EA, United Kingdom
80 McKenzie Street, Cape Town 8001, South Africa
Unit 1, 66 Gibbes Street, Chatswood, NSW 2067, Australia
218 Lake Road, Northcote, Auckland, New Zealand

A catalogue record for this book is available from
the British Library

ISBN 978 1 84773 940 7

This book was conceived, designed, and produced by
Ivy Press

Creative Director: Peter Bridgewater
Publisher: Jason Hook
Art Director: Wayne Blades
Senior Editor: Jayne Ansell
Designer: Clare Barber
Authors: Viv Croot & Jane Moseley
Illustrator: David Janes
Picture Researcher: Katie Greenwood
Cipher Consultant: Strabo Gaetanus

Cover credit: Bruce Amos/Fotolia

Printed in China
Colour origination by Ivy Press Reprographics

10 9 8 7 6 5 4 3 2 1

THE

MORIARTY

PAPERS

Compiled By Colonel Sebastian Moran

*The Adventures of Sherlock Holmes's
Great Nemesis*

NEW
HOLLAND

Publisher's Note

IN THIS VOLUME ARE THE ONLY SURVIVING PAPERS of Professor James Moriarty, one of the most enigmatic and mysterious of master criminals ever to stalk the annals of British history, and arch and mortal enemy of the eminent consulting detective, Sherlock Holmes.

The collection is itself a facsimile, a faithful reprint of the contemporary volume put out by Colonel Sebastian Moran under the aegis of Morris, Meatjay, circa 1915. It is believed that this was a publishing house owned by Professor Moriarty, but it fell into liquidation after his mysterious disappearance at the beginning of World War I.

Professor James Moriarty

An attempt by Moran to recoup his losses after the departure of his mentor and paymaster, the original version appeared to be a collection of papers, ephemera and documents; pages from Moriarty's diary, drawings, jottings, sketches and other material pertaining to the Professor's missions, along with worksheets from the cases that he engineered, most of which appear to have involved Sherlock Holmes, with whom Moriarty was obsessed. They are all that is left from a fire in premises at

Butcher Street that were later proven to be Moriarty's headquarters. Colonel Moran seems to have gathered up what he could, but he did not sort the material in any coherent order, chronological or otherwise; neither had his publishers done so.

When the original volume came to us we debated whether to reorganise it in a more logical manner; but given its nature and the condition in which it came to us, it was decided in the end to leave it in its original state. We feel confident that this collection, however incomplete and unorthodox in its presentation, will delight, intrigue and fascinate in equal measure.

> ### MORAN, SEBASTIAN, COL.
>
> Unemployed. Formerly 1st Bengalore Pioneers.
> BORN: London, 1840.
> Son of Sir Augustus Moran, C.B., once British Minister to Persia.
> EDUCATED: Eton and Oxford.
> SERVED in Jowaki Campaign (1877–8), Second Anglo–Afghan Campaign, Charasiab (1879; despatches), Sherpur (1879), and Cabul.
> AUTHOR of *Heavy Game of the Western Himalayas*, 1881; *Three Months in the Jungle*, 1884.
> ADDRESS: Conduit Street, London.
> CLUBS: The Anglo–Indian, the Tankerville, the Bagatelle Card Club, London.

Even with this rich research resource at our fingertips, and after much and repeated inspection, investigation and even dissection, we are still unable to establish the true identity of the elusive, quixotic Moriarty. We can make educated guesses at it, attempt calculated stabs at resolving the enigma, draw our conclusions about the truth of it, but that is all. There may be clues that we have missed, so we leave it to you to draw a final conclusion about this great literary mystery.

Sherlock Holmes

Irene in her prime on stage

Phrenology Head

Diogenes Club

MYCROFT HOLMES
Co-Founder

Found these stuffed in a cigar box

I find myself in an embarrassing situation now that Professor Moriarty, the visionary mastermind, is no more, or at least probably is no more (that man is a genius, I would not put it past him to be plotting something somewhere, running tests on his ant farm). Now that I'm down £6,000 per annum, I'm very low on tin, and spreading the boards ain't keeping me in good cigars, so I am hoping to get some reward from this little offering.

A cove's got to live. I've put together what's left of the Professor's papers found at our old HQ at 111c Butcher Street (there was a mysterious fire, I was out of town at the time). You'll have to excuse the chaos, I'm a Man of Action, never did take to the fiddly stuff.

Col. Sebastian Moran

Detection is, or ought to be, an exact science and should be treated in the same cold and unemotional manner. You have attempted to tinge it with romanticism, which produces much the same effect as if you worked a love story. Some facts should be suppressed, or, at least, a just sense of proportion should be observed in treating them. The only point in the case which deserved mention was the curious analytical reasoning from effects to causes, by which I succeeded in unravelling it.

November 20, 1887

Holmes has got the hack doctor Doyle to write up his part in the solving of the Mormon murders. It was one of my lesser successes. Drebber and Stangerson were endangering our Utah operation, but it was simplicity itself to bamboozle Holmes with misinformation that led him to blame Brigham Young for the killings, kicking up a fine diversionary dust storm. I look at him describing his precious so-called "method", the insufferable show-off. Fortunately, Sam Beeton is in hock to one of our racing gangs, so it was not difficult to persuade him to buy Doyle's story for a mere £25, flat fee, no royalties! Put that in your pipe, Sherlock!

Quack, quack

PRICE ONE SHILLING.

BEETON'S CHRISTMAS ANNUAL

A STUDY IN SCARLET

By A. CONAN DOYLE

Containing · also
Two Original
DRAWING ROOM PLAYS.
I.
FOOD FOR POWDER
By R. ANDRE
2
THE FOUR LEAVED SHAMROCK
By C. J. HAMILTON

With ENGRAVINGS
By D. H. FRISTON
MATT. STRETCH,
AND
R. ANDRÉ

WARD · LOCK & CO
LONDON · NEW · YORK
AND · MELBOURNE ·

SH/ASIS/1881:
THE TWO PILLS EXPERIMENT
✳ ✳ ✳

MISSION: to silence Enoch Drebber and Joseph Stangerson who had betrayed the Moriarty clan; as a secondary aim to blind test moriartium in pill form

Drebber and Stangerson had besmirched the Moriarty name when they stole from our unregistered silver mines in Utah in the 1840s. Our inside man was Jefferson Hope; I arranged temporary employ for him at York College, Pennsylvania and instructed him in rudimentary dispensing. Once he had the moriartium pills and what he thought were placebos, he tracked these two repellent oafs all over the Americas and Europe, finally pinning them down in Brixton. It was thus that I first encountered the egregious Holmes; dressed as the crone Sawyer, I was easily able to outwit the insufferable prig using an ancient cab dodging trick. Ha! However, was quite impressed when he used a magnifying glass; thought I had the only one in the country. Made sure Hope never went to trial; Watson diagnosed an aortic aneurysm, but what does he know?

NOTE I: Doyle/the dolt Watson put in all that sickly saccharine nonsense about Lucy Ferrier, "the love of Hope's life", presumably to attract the lady readers. Doyle is a terrible one for the ladies. He also decided on that dreadful title. "Scarlet thread of murder". Hack.

NOTE 2: Moriartium pills worked perfectly; Stangerson died in an instant.

GRIM REAPER TAKES MORMON

OUR CORRESPONDENT

The public have lost a sensational treat through the sudden death of the man Hope, who was suspected of the murder of Mr. Enoch Drebber and of Mr. Joseph Stangerson. The details of the case will probably be never known now, though we are informed upon good authority that the crime was the result of an old-standing and romantic feud, in which love and Mormonism bore a part. It seems that both the victims belonged, in their younger days, to the Latter Day Saints, and Hope, the deceased prisoner, hails also from Salt Lake City. If the case has had no other effect, it, at least, brings out in the most striking manner the efficiency of our detective police force, and will serve as a lesson to all foreigners that they will do wisely to settle their feuds at home, and not to carry them on to British soil. It is an open secret that the credit of this smart capture belongs entirely to the well-known Scotland Yard officials, Messrs.

GUION LINE

STEAMSHIP TICKET

THIRD CLASS

★

MO 1A

This is the MO 1A, it's unique and mine, how the devil did Holmes get hold of it?

April 28, 1891

Holmes thinks he is on the point of unmasking me, and putting my entire operation under the hammer of the law. He isn't of course, the law does not apply to such as I, and of course I saw every step which he took to draw his toils around me, but he is discommoding and tiresome; just listen to him whine on, self-justification and sheer terror oozing from every pore: "but I could not rest, Watson, I could not sit quiet in my chair, if I thought that such a man as Professor Moriarty were walking the streets of London unchallenged." I plan to give him a scare, the arrogant imbecile. I shall visit him in his own sordid rooms, just to show I know where he lives. Mrs Hudson has given me a key and will find a pressing engagement elsewhere, and the hooligan rabble that are the Baker Street Irregulars will find themselves inconveniently ambushed by their Butcher Street counterparts.

I appeared, silent and malevolent, on his doorstep, catching him by surprise, sitting there in his ridiculous dressing gown. His rooms are unspeakable, like those of a first-year medical student: littered with syringes, pipes, broke-back books, papers, tobacco shreds — and the bedroom wall smothered in portraits of my colleagues in crime. Unnerving. As I had the element of surprise, I struck first. "You have less frontal development than I should have expected," I sneered, and pointed out that the revolver he had in his pocket would go off if he did not stop fingering it. I was sweet reason itself. "You crossed my path on the 4th of January," I told him. "On the 23rd you incommoded me; by the middle of February I was seriously inconvenienced by you; at the end of March I was absolutely hampered in my plans; and now, at the close of April, I find myself placed in such a position through your continual persecution that I am in positive danger of losing my liberty." Then I slid in the threat, like a stiletto into a wound, buttering him up first. "It has been an intellectual treat to me to see the way in which you have grappled with this affair, and I say, unaffectedly, that it would be a grief to me to be forced to take any extreme measure. You smile, sir, but I assure you that it really would. If you are clever enough to bring destruction upon me, rest assured that I shall do as much to you." I don't think I could have been clearer.

April 29, 1891

Followed through sending out my most subtly crafty henchmen to appear to run him down with a two-horse van, to smash his head in with a brick and to beat him senseless with a bludgeon. The witless oaf thinks he escaped by his own agility and pugilistic prowess. Hubris! Now I have him on the run to the continent where it will be simple for Moran and self to dispatch him, away from the prying eyes of those few officials of the law I have not managed to suborn.

May 15th. 1882

Dear Sir

I am not surprised at your friend's anger, but he and you should know that to denounce the murders was the only course open to us. To do that promptly was plainly our best policy. But you can tell him, and all others concerned, that, though I regret the accident of Lord Frederick Cavendish's death, I cannot refuse to admit that Burke got no more than his deserts. You are at liberty to show him this, and others whom you can trust also, but let not my address be known. He can write to House of Commons.

Yours very truly,

Chas. S. Parnell.

United States Patent Office

JAMES A. FOSTER, OF DETROIT, MICHIGAN.

Letters Patent No. 92,031, dated June 29, 1869.

IMPROVED ARTIFICIAL LEG.

The Schedule referred to in these Letters Patent and making part of the same.

To whom it may concern:

Be it known that I, JAMES A. FOSTER, of Detroit, in the county of Wayne, and State of Michigan, have invented a new and useful Improvement in Artificial Legs; and I do declare that the following is a true and accurate description thereof, reference being had to the accompanying drawings, and to the letters of reference marked thereon, and being a part of this specification.

Figure 1 is a vertical section, showing the interior arrangement of the parts forming the operating-parts of the leg.

Figure 2 is a plan view of my hollow knee-bolt and its attachments.

of juncture form........ the two parts together.

D is a wood........
bolt A partially........

E is an eye........
which encloses........
posite end of........
is provided w........
of which the........
adjusted, and the wear........
for.

The straps or plates B and C extend downwa........ and are secured to the inferior leg, as sh........

Rembrandt

Moriarty's forgeries; bally good, if you ask me, but apparently unsaleable, dammit

150
135
120
105
90
75
60
45
30
15
0

SHIP BEYOND THE HORIZON

...MAMENT

	MAX. ELEV.	RANGE
... CAL TWIN TURRETS	35°	32,500 YD.
... CAL AA TWIN SHIELD MOUNTS	85°	18,000 YD.
... CAL AA (REPORTED)	85°	9,900 YD.
...RPEDO TUBES (TRIPLE MOUNTS)		
...ULTS—4 SEAPLANE SCOUTS		
...CHARGES CARRIED		

PROTECT...

BELT—2¼"
TURRETS—
BARBETTES—
CONNING TOWE...
DECKS—2"
(OVER V...

Cape Me Si Potes

Napoleon

Arthur Conan Doyle

Pictorialis

SH/TASH/OI/I888:
THE BOHEMIAN ULTIMATUM

***

MISSION: to extract money from the King of Bohemia
(death to all kings!) to fulfil an urgent and pressing
need for funds

This should have been a foolproof fundraising
event. My minion, and twin sister in devious evil,
Irene Adler, the banshee from New Jersey who is
nevertheless a magnet for men, especially rich
and stupid ones, was a natural. She had limed her
mark in Warsaw, and now the scheme was coming
to fruition as the royal dolt was getting married,
and she had a compromising photograph (I had taken
it with my Kodak box camera, a wonderful device,
which apparently cannot lie). I taught her all she
knows, so it was no great surprise, but a trifle
disappointing, that she cheated me, married her
lawyer and left the country with the photograph as
insurance. Treachery, thy name is woman.

NOTES: A botched mission, but it was reward enough
to watch the eagle-eyed one completely fail to
recognise me lounging about in the mob he had hired
for his ridiculous fake fire alarm; and to see Adler
penetrate his pathetic "disguise" and trump him
without even taking off her gloves. A bonus is that
he has fallen in love with the conniving harlot!
I saw his great moony face: no hard cash but a rich
seam of schadenfreude, and an exploitable weakness
at the heart of Holmes.

June 6, 1890

I hate him. I hate him. I burn with loathing at the mere thought of his existence. He was a nobody until I took him up; nothing but a pale reflection of my superior genius, a feeble, slavish Little Sir Echo: the gaunt frame, the imposing height, the domed forehead indicating (wrongly in his case) a mighty brain, the military henchman of dim wattage. Yet he is in EVERY PARTICULAR my inferior: he does not even know that the Earth orbits the Sun. I am a bona fide man of science who has published a serious trail-blazing study on higher mathematics, acclaimed by the intelligentsia of all Europe; he is an unofficial consulting detective who scrawls ridiculous monographs on cigar ash and wastes his time compiling a pathetic Encyclopedia of Criminals. I have an original Greuze on my wall; he has a likeness of the Queen which he uses for target practice. I am a master of impenetrable disguise; he has a facile ability to pass himself off as somebody else (at least enough to fool Watson, not the greatest of intellectual challenges). Yet whose name is on everyone's lips? Thanks to Doyle's plausible hackery, it is that of Holmes. His arrogant self-satisfied platitudinising is more than a man of sense can bear: "When you have eliminated the impossible, whatever remains, however improbable, must be the truth" indeed. What will he come up with next? An insight into how much more useful is a wall if it can only be induced to maintain perpendicularity?

But how to deal with this corrosive loathing that clouds my mind and makes the detailed planning of missions an impossibility? I turn to the arts, and express my rage through the healing medium of collage. It is not the perfect solution, but it has a strangely therapeutic effect.

July 17, 1889

Heads will roll. If I hadn't ploughed through Doyle's cumbersome prose I would never have discovered how close SH came to ruining our Swandam Operation. Doyle laps up all Watson tells him but who would have thought he would write up this story: there's no crime or criminal, it's just one stupendous piece of puffery for the Sage of Baker Street.

It was all down to Watson. Must keep a closer eye, even though I have married him off to one of the Marys (she doesn't think much of him, can't even remember his name) he occasionally slips the leash. One night in June, he toddled off to the opium den "to rescue a friend" and there he met Sherlock "on a case". In an unusual access of acumen, Watson went along with it, in case it was one of ours. (Fortunately Holmes is an arrogant solipsist who would never question why a newly wedded man would turn down a warm night in the marital bed to dash off into the night with a bachelor friend.)

Piecing it together from Doyle's clunking prose, I deduce (I can do this sort of thing too) that Holmes had blundered into Hughie "The Lip" Boone's little enterprise. Boone had been on the payroll for some five years as a Fleet Street insider; when he turned to more lucrative begging, I saw no reason to change our arrangement; information was passed during his banter with passersby, and his collecting hat served as a drop-off point for coded messages. He got a stipend and was allowed to keep whatever went into his hat (after a deduction for expenses). As he has the gift of the gab, he was soon coining it, but instead of keeping quiet and salting it away, what does he do but set himself up in a suburban villa with a fluffy little wife, and call himself Neville St Clair! He has such a banal mind. I did not discourage him because it gave me a stronger hold over him, and he could legitimately lodge in the opium den and keep an eye on the Lascar, who I was certain was skimming the profits, to fund his own nefarious enterprise.

I am prepared to believe it was pure coincidence that Boone's wife happened to see him in the den, leading to his arrest as the murderer of his alter ego (smart thinking on Boone's part). The determined baggage set Holmes on the trail. After much cogitation and an ounce of shag, H finally cottoned on that Boone and St Clair were one and the same (so much for his powers of observation), and did one of his theatrical reveals, wiping Boone's face to reveal St Clair in the presence of the might of the law. Our man on the force, Bradstreet, stood by ready with his nightstick but there was no need. Once again, Holmes failed to follow through, so intent was he on looking omniscient and magnanimous, pointing out that there was no crime so no criminal, and walking off looking pleased with himself. Vanity, vanity, all is vanity.

SH/TASH/05/1887:
THE KKK EXPERIMENT
***

MISSION: to bring the KKK to its knees; a Moriarty cannot tolerate a rival organisation overreaching him in terms of evil

The experiment was perfectly set up; Elias Openshaw's success in the Confederate Army and as a planter was guaranteed by my machinations, so he was in no position to refuse when I ordered him to steal the incriminating diary and register from the KKK headquarters in March '69. All we had to do was wait; I can play a long game. Minions followed the idiotic young John Openshaw, and as soon as I learnt of the setting of the pips (vulgar but effective, typically American), I used the Colonel Prendergast identity to nudge him towards Holmes. The idea was for Holmes to expose the organisation, so that the Moriarty connection would go completely unrecognised. Of course he failed utterly (although you would not know it from Doyle's account). All Openshaws dead, including the smug bicycle king, and still no KKK exposure; Holmes was intolerably obtuse; even Watson guessed the murderers were on a ship. Finally had to scuttle the operation (and the **Lone Star**) myself, using the Swedish mercenaries the fool Captain Calhoun had taken on board.

NOTES: A satisfactory outcome, but neither neat nor elegant; Holmes showed himself the puffed up incompetent he actually is. Impressed by the KKK uniforms; maybe adjust to fit my purposes?

The Moriarty All-in-One Concealer (Prototype I)

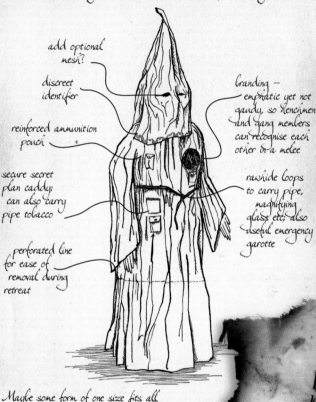

add optional mesh?

discreet identifier

reinforced ammunition pouch

secure secret plan caddy; can also carry pipe tobacco

perforated line for ease of removal during retreat

branding — emphatic yet not gaudy, so henchmen and gang members can recognise each other in a melee

rawhide loops to carry pipe, magnifying glass etc; also useful emergency garrotte

Maybe some form of one size fits all uniform would improve gang morale?

June 15, 1890

I blame Doyle. He cannot write, but like all doctors he thinks he is a Renaissance man. He boasts of dashing off his first "adventure" in less than three weeks, as if it is not more than apparent that it was scrawled in haste by a cocksure amateur. Perhaps he deserves some slight recognition for wrangling Watson's inchoate ramblings into an order of sorts, even if they are full of anachronisms and elementary inaccuracies. Yet the idiot public lap up his tawdry scribblings and now he's got an American publisher. And even though Holmes would be nothing without me, and I am the motive force behind his "adventures" (conceive how tedious they would be if I weren't), I get barely a mention.

And he simply glosses over the times when I annihilate Holmes entirely: what of the sheer logistical magnificence of the Camberwell poisonings? The very lucrative Amateur Mendicant Society? The undoing of the egregious Grice Patersons? How and why the Sophy Anderson went down? What went on in the Paradol Chamber? Matilda Griggs and the Giant Rat of Sumatra? A bare mention by the traducer Watson, and then dismissed as too jejune to narrate. I have sent Doyle a stiff letter, which I believe has shaken him; I am determined to be recognised as the man I am, to be delineated in the respectful manner I deserve... something like "the Napoleon of crime" would go some way to appeasing my rage, but it would still be too little, Doyle, and too late.

Professor James Moriarty

To A.C. Doyle MD
Tennison Road
Norwood , S.E.

June 15, 1890

Sir,
  My lawyers inform me that you are the amanuensis of
Dr John Watson and are bringing to public attention the
adventures of his eccentric, drug-addled colleague,
Sherlock Holmes. My name is apparently mentioned in some
of these works, and in many cases my character besmirched
in a derogatory manner.
        I can find no record of your having done me the courtesy
of requesting permission to use my name in your publications
to date. Allow me therefore to take the liberty of informing you
that unless my name is either expunged from your writings
or I am represented in my true light, and any description,
delineation, reference, mention or discussion of my person,
character or actions is read and amended if necessary by me
before publication, I shall be instructing my lawyers to take
the most vigorous legal action as a matter of urgency.
        I await your response, sir, within the soonest
possible period,

                          James Moriarty

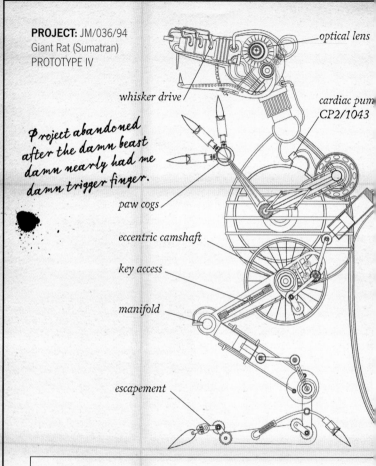

PROJECT: JM/036/94
Giant Rat (Sumatran)
PROTOTYPE IV

optical lens

whisker drive

cardiac pump
CP2/1043

Project abandoned after the damn beast damn nearly had me damn trigger finger.

paw cogs

eccentric camshaft

key access

manifold

escapement

SPECIFICATIONS
CLIENT: JM
MATERIALS: copper, steel, leather, rodent integuement
DIMENSIONS: l 32 ins;
h at shoulder 12 ins; girth 5 ins

OPTIMUM BELLY: 22 ins
MOTIVE POWER: clockwork/steam Swiss standard twin pocket watch drive, with escapement

Sundamys Infraluteus

February 2, 1891

I am currently engaged on an intriguing side project; the work is still at a sensitive stage, so I am recording results in my diary rather than creating a file for public record. The science of phrenology has lost favour recently, but I believe that is because lax minds use it as a toy. (Even intolerable Holmes has got a phrenology bust in his sordid apartments, I saw it on my visit there; he fondles it as if he knows what he is doing; all he has ever deduced is that a person in possession of a large head must have a large brain within; his own oversized cranium should prove what a fallacy this is.)

I have studied the master, Franz Joseph Gall and conclude that of the 27 organs he proposes, many can be enhanced or diminished. Some pioneering experimentation using small hammers, hot and cold compresses, a miniature vice, mild electric currents and willing volunteers who are happy to offer themselves to the advancement of science in return for my not evicting them from their hovels have helped me prove that some of the more useful brain areas can be amplified. I have also developed a set of exercises, a slow masticating motion made as the lower jaw is swung from side to side through a small arc, in the manner of a boa constrictor; this routine helps to dissolve muscular tension that would otherwise interfere with vital cogitation. I am certain that it stimulates brain areas 9 and 27, but am still collecting data.

The Moriarty Superbrain

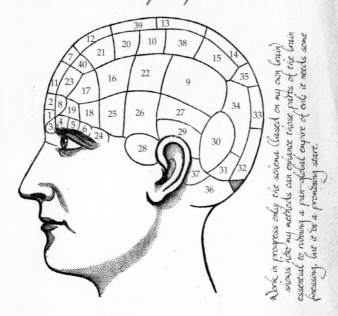

Work in progress only the scheme (based on my own brain) shows how my methods can enhance those parts of the brain essential to reducing a pan-global empire of evil. It needs some finessing, but it is a promising start.

KEY TO SUPERBRAIN

Amplified brain organs are marked by two stars; diminished organs are marked by one star

1. Sexual desire
2. Children *
3. Friendship*
4. Aggression **
5. Homicidal tendency**
6. Devious cunning**
7. Thievery**
8. Arrogance **
9. Ruthless ambition**
10. Strategy**
11. Memory for detail**
12. Timing**
13. People's weaknesses**
14. Vocabulary
15. Language
16. Colour
17. Sound
18. Numbers**
19. Engineering**
20. Cleverness**
21. Scientific method**
22. Wit**
23. Poetry*
24. Kindness*
25. Mimicry and disguise**
26. Religion*
27. Inflexibility of purpose**

I have established 13 other areas of the brain that Gall failed to discover, but have not yet decided how they are to be allocated

THE FORMICOPHILIA SOCIETY OF TRALEE
THE METROPOLIS FORMICARIUM FSF 1890/A

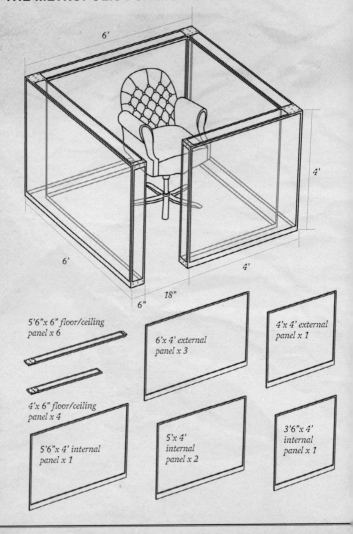

6'

4'

4'

6'

4'

6"

18"

5'6"x 6" floor/ceiling
panel x 6

6'x 4' external
panel x 3

4'x 4' external
panel x 1

4'x 6" floor/ceiling
panel x 4

5'6"x 4' internal
panel x 1

5'x 4'
internal
panel x 2

3'6"x 4'
internal
panel x 1

ANT REQUIREMENTS

 500 X DRONES

5000 X WORKERS

1 X QUEEN

THE FORMICOPHILIA SOCIETY OF TRALEE

ESTABLISHED 1887

FORMIS HOUSE, TRALEE, CO. KERRY, EIRE

DATE: *March 17, 1890*

CLIENT ADDRESS: *Professor James Moriarty,*
11 le Butcher Street, London

TO: *Supplying plans for*
the "Metropolis" model
Ant Farm

RECEIVED WITH THANKS	£2	13	6

AERY SMIT (MAJOR)
PRESIDENT OF THE FORMICOPHILIA SOCIETY

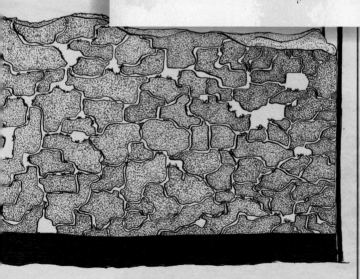

April 30, 1881

The individual calling himself Sherlock Holmes is beginning to encroach on my operations, and my nerves. I must admit it is intriguing: as arrogantly thick-headed as he is, he is a vast improvement on Moran as a strop for the razor of my finely edged mind. He obviously moulds himself on my template — he works with a network of informers and a melee of unruly ragamuffins called the Baker Street Irregulars (a mirror to our own Butcher Street Illiterati).

It will be simple to keep him under surveillance as he is now lodging in one of my properties (one of the Irregulars in my pay set him up) under the bovine gaze of Mrs Hudson. He does not suspect. It never occurs to him to wonder why his appalling behaviour does not induce her to hand in her notice or throw him out; he is a solipsist, devoid of a single social skill.

You would not think it to look at her, but Mrs H. was once the glorious Emmy "Ra-Ra" Joist, the queen of the Zeedijk soubrettes; I met her years ago when I was studying with Professor Strabismus in Amsterdam; she conceived a passion for me I could not return (she has no brain) but her list of admirers was a blackmailer's dream, so I married her off to the capon Humphrey Hudson and brought her to London. The current strain on Anglo-Dutch relations offers no challenge: she was always a passable actress and her Cockney accent is impeccable.

I informed cloaxK Iam't Emma ahd I did't blart the blighter's

met liefde,
Emmy "Ra-Ra"
Soist XXX

August 12, 1889

I had the dream again. This will be the third time.
Although my keen mind needs but few hours sleep and
I often cheat Morpheus by working through the night on
a particularly complicated venture, or the compiling of a
more than usually fiendish puzzle for the Cruciverbalist
Society, or improvising on my tambourine. It pains me to
admit even to my diary that this dream unnerves me.
It cannot be drug-induced: I eschew all forms of
brain-numbing influences. Look at Holmes and his
wretched seven percent solution.

I have just now awoken and will endeavour to record my
experience as accurately as I can. I drift off and then
suddenly it feels as if I am
awake in the real world, and
I find myself pinned to a divan,
a hookah full of what I fear is
the foul mind poison they call
yeti's marjoram nearby. I cannot
move or make myself understood
to anybody and yet I am
possessed of an unaccountable
restlessness. Days go past,
people loom at me — I think
I see the sap Watson at some
point. Then I fall asleep IN
THE DREAM and wake up

EDMUND
FRUSIG
Alienist

TELEGRAPH: HAMPSTEAD 321
LONDON VIENNA NEW YORK

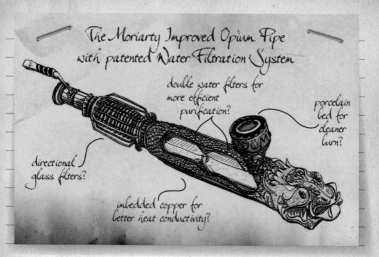

The Moriarty Improved Opium Pipe
with patented Water Filtration System

double water filters for
more efficient
purification?

porcelain
bed for
cleaner
burn?

directional
glass filters?

imbedded copper for
better heat conductivity?

in one of our opium dens; then it all goes black again,
and I wake up in my rooms when I am always thirsty
and famished and have to devour a woodcock or two.
Have made an appointment with Edmund Frusig the
alienist (I will not see Sigmund Freud, he is a friend
of Doyle's) to see if he can throw some light. It is
incommoding my operation and a criminal mastermind
has to be just that, a master of his own mind.

NB While in the dream opium den, I could not help
noticing that the pipes they used burn inefficiently;
they could be reconfigured to produce more derangement
using less opium while charging the same; I have a
made a rough design, it can go into production at our
Rotherhithe plant.

Fig. 14 Fig. 13 Fig. 20 Fig. 38
Fig. 16
Fig. 31
Fig. 6 Fig. 26 Fig. 27
Fig. 23 Fig. 24 Fig. 29 Fig. 28
Fig. 36
Fig. 2
Fig. 4
Fig. 3
Fig. 30

He spent a fortune on this stuff, the devil knows why; waste of good tin if you ask me.

December 24, 1891

Doyle has finally given my character some backing in his wretched hackery, but can he simply let my dark genius shine out like an obsidian beacon to all that is glitteringly evil and malevolent? Am I allowed to properly inhabit the role of nemesis, arch enemy, the one true Napoleon of crime (as he was forced to call me after several more uncompromising communications from my lawyers, Moire, Jay & Smart)? No. I get a paragraph or two, and then the Smug One starts to bleat about Jonathan Wild, an 18th-century entrepreneur.

My research indicates that Wild was indeed a man after my own heart who really made crime pay — occupying the role of thief taker and thief in one smooth and highly lucrative operation. No bad thing, but this comparison set Doyle's illiterate admirers off; now they conceive that I am a fictional construct and all manner of theories seep out of their perfervid imaginations. Could I be based on Adam Worth, a German-born American who was very successful until that ill-thought-out disaster in Belgium? Plausible, but simply not in my class. Some lunatics believed that because I know a reflective telescope from a handsaw I must be based on Mad-Dog Newcomb, the belligerent stargazer; a small group of diehard ignoramuses even cite poor tedious old Truth Functional Boole, a man of mathematics but no magnetism. What an uninspiring crew; I am so much more than the sum of all these.

An uninspiring crew

Jonathan Wild 1683–1725

Adam Worth 1844–

George Boole 1815–1864

Simon Newcomb 1835–

SH/TASH/08/1883:
THE SNAKEBITE OPTION

***

MISSION: to assassinate Holmes by means of moriartium administered via mechanical snake to give the appearance of an unfortunate accident

I set up the scheme in Stoke Moran, a battered ruin belonging to one of the Colonel's reprobate relations. I thought it a sporting clue for Holmes, but, obtuse as he is arrogant, he made no connection. Moran didn't tell me until the game was afoot that he kept a cheetah and baboon there for shooting practice — but it added to the atmosphere. Grimesby Roylott was an oafish blackguard but owed me money and jumped at the chance of writing it off; the Stoner twins are always up for an adventure — a pity about Miss Julia, she was a useful minx, but that was Roylott; I did tell him to use valerian on the dummy run. All going to plan, Watson putting his Eley No 2 just out of reach, but at the last minute Holmes managed with a lucky flail of his cane to throw the device back up through the ventilator.

NOTES: The serpentine device worked well, but must reconfigure the snake to respond to a specific whistle code. Idiot Holmes did not even realise it was a trick snake, so much for his mighty brain and ability to identify every beetle under the sun. "A Swamp Adder, the deadliest snake in India!" Ha! Roylott no loss, although had to write off debt.

Mark 1 Swamp Adder

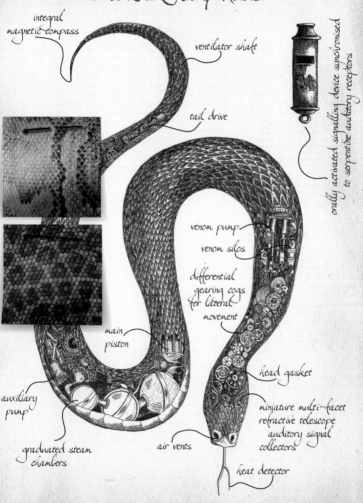

integral magnetic compass

ventilator shaft

tail drive

orally activated signalling device synchronised to serpentine auditory receptors

venom pump

venom silos

differential gearing cogs for lateral movement

main piston

head gasket

auxiliary pump

miniature multi-facet refractive telescope auditory signal collectors

graduated steam chambers

air vents

heat detector

September 15, 1890

No Napoleon can do without his marshals, and I of course have my constabulary contacts. Their role is to destabilize the Arrogant One to the best of their abilities, report his every action to me, and to misplace clues, misdirect information and make every case harder for him, so that I can watch him struggle. For this they are amply remunerated.

It is time for my annual review of their performances; they all have their different methods, some more successful than others. Lestrade continues to shine, I knew his sallow, rat-like appearance would lull Holmes into a false sense of security — vain men consistently rely on physiognomy rather than action as a pointer to success (Note: rein Lestrade in? He may be getting above himself). Toby Gregson does a convincing line in oleaginous grovelling. "I would esteem it a great kindness if you would favour me with your opinion." Masterful. Gregory's procedural competence unnerves Holmes, so he sneers that the man has no imagination and doesn't stop to consider that Gregory might be destroying evidence. Bradstreet (an ex-Bow Street Runner) is ever reliable; no one would suspect that perfidy would lurk behind those mutton chops. Peter Jones has perfected damning with faint praise ("He has his own little methods"), guaranteed to make H angry and therefore careless. Jones's cousin Athelney has made the "imbecile" role his own. Baynes of the Surrey force was a great find, provoking self-congratulatory condescension in H that once again made him careless. And young Stanley Hopkins simply aped the Sherlock "method", flattering the enormous Sherlockian ego so that he ceased to pay attention to the case. But the bonus this year must go once again to Inspector Alex MacDonald; he caused Holmes to love and adore him by appearing all dour and Scottish and trustworthy, subtly allowing Holmes to condescend outrageously (I do not know how he stands it); Inspector Mac has him so besotted that he can even tell him that the CID think that he has a bee in his bonnet about me, and that I am but a harmless astronomer, and still the Panjandrum of Baker Street did not take offence. Superlative work.

September 9, 1888

The annual meeting of the Ó Muircheartaigh clan and all its septs, at the usual secret rendezvous. What a slew of incompetent, idle malefactors, lunatics, gannets and drunkards! Surely they are not my kin — there can be fewer than 20 brain cells between them; I am beginning to wonder whether forking out once a year to feed their fat faces is money well spent; but an evil empire won't run itself, this is an efficient way to show that I know where they all live, and when it comes to loyal henchmen, blood is, literally, thicker than water.

High Table

Professor James Moriarty
Colonel James Moriarty
Giacomo Moriati
Jean-Jacques Moriarté
Jacobus Moriartie
Diego Moriarty y Torres
Osvaldo Moriarty y Suarez
Jakob Jakobbson Moriarty
Dmitri Yakovitch Moriarty
Moriarty Jiming
Moriarty Jeimuzu
Jake Goolagong Moriarty
James Pierrepoint Moriarty Jnr.
Jaap Jaapzoon Moriartie
Hamish Moriarty
Bernardo Moriarty y Higgins
Ernesto Moriarty y Lynch
Molly McGuire Moriarty
Mary Moriarty
Mary Bernardette Moriarty
Mary Annunciata Moriarty
Mary Dolores Mercedes Moriarty
Seamus Ó Muircheartaigh
Cathleen ni Houlihan
Ó Muircheartaigh
Colonel Sebastian
Moran Moriarty
Wolfe Tone Moriarty

Guest Tables

The O'Donoghues The O'Mahonys

Moran can't deny the family tie, and I've got a couple of fetching second cousins (both called Mary) lined up for Watson, the uxorious bonehead.

REMY JASMORAIT & CIE
Marchands des Vins
St James W.I.
LONDRES PARIS
Macon Tralee

Moran!!

POUR L'ATTENTION DE: M. le Professeur Moriarty

10 x case	Nuits St Georges 1874
10 x case	Chablis 1er Cru Les Fys 1872
10 x case	Bourgogne Pinot Noir 1877
10 x case	Côtes de Beaune Villages 1879
10 x case	Meursault Puligny Montrachet 1865
12 x case	Château Lynch Bages Grand Cru 1868
12 x case	Gevrey Chambertin 1er Cru 1860
24 bottles	Hennessy Cognac
12 x case	Champagne Laurent Perrier 1887
12 x case	Champagne Roederer Cristal 1876
12 x case	Moët & Chandon Brut Imperial 1865
12 x case	Champagne Veuve Clicquot 1872
12 x case	Champagne Pol Roger 1884

a rendre: One thousand guineas

THE GATHERING OF THE O'MUIRCHEARTAIGH

SEPTEMBER 1888

Professor James Moriarty

MOTTO: SCANDIT SUBLIMA VIRTUS

Osvaldo Moriarty y Suarez from the Bolivian branch is not in attendance; ominous.

95

SH/TASH/02/I890:
THE JOHN CLAY INITIATIVE
* * *

MISSION: to requisition 30,000 napoleons of French gold from the Coburg Square branch of the City and Suburban Bank in London

This was Clay's initiative test: I wanted to see if he could play Berthier to my Napoleon. A bright young man of imagination, invention and initiative, but sadly delusional (he was convinced he was wrong-side-of-the-blanket royal) but did attend Eton and Oxford, who can be relied upon to turn out a decent gentleman criminal (look at Moran). It was diverting, choking Fleet Street with red-headed men to winkle idiotic pawnbroker out of his sordid but strategic shop (Moran looked a sight); did not think Wilson would have the initiative to go to Holmes, but it added a frisson. Any halfway competent sleuth would have seen through the plot in an instant but Doyle dressed it up as a three-pipe-problem to make SH look good. He got there in the end, most vexing, and Clay will be dancing the hemp fandango.

NOTES: May be able to establish lucrative market for the red hair dye. Fortunately Holmes did not examine the artificial knee enterprise in King Edward Street very closely (he is a slack-minded complacent) so our diamond-smuggling operation remains uncompromised.

FLAME RED HAIR IMPROVER

* * *

INGREDIENTS

Flowers of sulphur ... $1/2$ ounce
Glycerine ... I ounce
Rectified spirits of wine
... $1/2$ ounce
Pure Arabian Henna powder
... I ounce
Dried, crushed beetroot
... 2 ounces
Cochineal ... 4 drops
Arsenic ... 0.005 grain
Rosewater ... 8 ounces

METHOD

* Combine henna and dried beetroot with flowers of sulphur on a glass plate.
*In a ceramic bowl mix glycerine, rosewater and spirits of wine, and add cochineal.
* Using a wooden spoon, add dry ingredients to wet and stir until thoroughly emulsified.
* Wearing gloves, add arsenic (for extra shine).
* Allow to stand for 24 hours in a cool place then store in a dark glass jar with cork stopper. Use within one week.

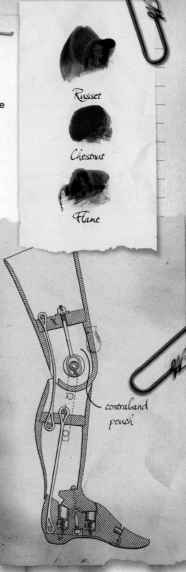

Russet

Chestnut

Flame

contraband pouch

***

MISSION: to steal the blue carbuncle belonging
to the Countess of Morcar to complete my set of
unusually coloured precious stones

Getting hold of the Morcar Carbuncle was a matter
of **amour-propre**. Its azure stare entranced me.
I'd already been obliged to arrange a couple of
accelerated deaths and some robberies in pursuit
of it, and still the elusive sparkler remained
tantalisingly outside the Moriarty vault. So when
second cousin Kitty Cusack telegraphed me to say
that she and her mistress (the Countess) would be
at the Hotel Cosmopolitan at Christmas, it was
carpe diem. She wanted her cut, the treacherous
wench, but it would be worth it; I turned over in my
mind the thought of holding the thing to ransom, as
the countess — a tediously emotional and indiscreet
woman — would pay half her considerable fortune
just to get it back. A pretty dilemma.

Unfortunately, the Christmas season (about which I
am at one with Scrooge) meant that I had to undertake
this endeavour with a less than adequate team;
even Moran was in Africa blasting away at lion.
I prevailed upon James Ryder, the pusillanimous
head attendant at the Hotel Cosmopolitan and one
of the lesser strings on our network of hotel snouts
who tip the wink when any jewel-rich imbeciles book
in. Ryder and Kitty lifted the shiner, setting up
John Horner as a catspaw. Ryder panicked (when will

I learn?) but then hit on what I have to admit is a brilliant idea; he went to his sister's goose-fattening establishment in Brixton, rammed the carbuncle down a bird's throat and carried it unnoticed through the streets of London to me (I used the Maudsley persona). Blind panic can be the mother of invention. We dug around in that bird's innards for at least 20 minutes before it became obvious that the wretched little worm had brought the wrong goose.

I tracked down the right goose, and the poor sap who bought it, and had my team of ruffians (the Butcher Street Illiterati) fall upon him at the corner of the Tottenham Court Rd; we would have had it, had not the commissionaire Peterson come on the scene and picked up the wretched anserine and Baker's hat; of course Doyle seized on that and wrote "a load of old hat" about Holmes deducing Baker's life story from it. Mrs Peterson found the carbuncle when she tried to cook the goose, and instead of pocketing it for the reward, the forelock-tugging sycophant handed it back to Holmes!

NOTES: Book Ryder's passage to Tierra del Fuego along with Kitty Cusack. Tip off Scotland Yard that Holmes has been perverting the course of justice by allowing criminals to go free. And where, oh where, is my cerulean darling now?

December 5, 1888

You know, I weary of the world of man. The human race is lazy, venal, ungrateful, perfidious and unreliable; how much more profitable it is to study the animal kingdom. I have ordered a new formicarium from The Formicophilia Society of Tralee, of which I am quondam president. Moran can build it, and it will please me to watch the eager little insects scurry about, responding instantly to every change I make to their environment; I shall sit motionless at the centre of their world like a great spider, in complete control, directing their lives on a whim. I can do this with humans, of course, but I find it takes so much longer and there are always troublemakers.

Bending my great brain to more mechanical matters, I have conceived of a revolutionary new weapon, based on high-frequency sound waves. Barely off the drawing board, it is extremely effective over a short range (hence the need for a new formicarium but unfortunately devours power. I envisage it will be very useful to the organisation, and will command a great price in the relevant circles, as it can be activated from afar by a whistle and, if strategically placed, can cause a great deal of damage, including the deafening of any guard dogs. It has demonstrated a curious side effect, however: Moran always carries a supply of Herr Daniel Peter's new Swiss Milk Chocolate (he claims it is to keep his brain alert while sniping, but he has always had a

Bally thing cost me 4 guineas for a new wescoat!!

shockingly sweet tooth) and the weapon appears to have the capacity to melt it at 100 paces while leaving surrounding buildings intact. Cannot adduce what use this might be, but have logged it in my report. May need to call in von Herder. My engineers, Rami Ramjets Oy, are meticulous, but being Finnish are martyrs to gloom and are prone to find only disaster where more enterprising intelligences see opportunity.

I have also started preliminary work on a new, improved hansom cab, which I conceive will make our operation invincible. It will appear to the dull eyes of the hoi polloi just another "London gondola", but my plan is to conceal within its frame a number of devices and machineries that will enable it to run fully armed yet undetected around the city; I toy with the notion of an amphibian element, so that the river is no longer an obstacle. And maybe some form of mobile telegraph.

Also spent some time rearranging my catalogue of disguises. Holmes may delude himself that he can pull off some convincing mummery, but he is always complaining that it causes physical pain. He is in this, as everything else, a posturing dilettante. My camouflage is impeccably impenetrable, I have perfected the art of total illusion, the power of my mind fooling people into seeing what I want them to see. It's the kind of mind trick that the Deer—Stalkered show—off will never come close to achieving.

The Moriarty Non-Ballistic Recoil-less Telesonar Pacifier

Blasted thing melted Mrs H's chocolate macaroons and boiled me whiskey

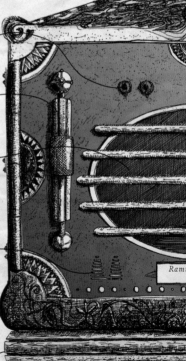

directional governor

delay device

dampers

monitor window

temperature gauge

amphibian tracks

Rami
H

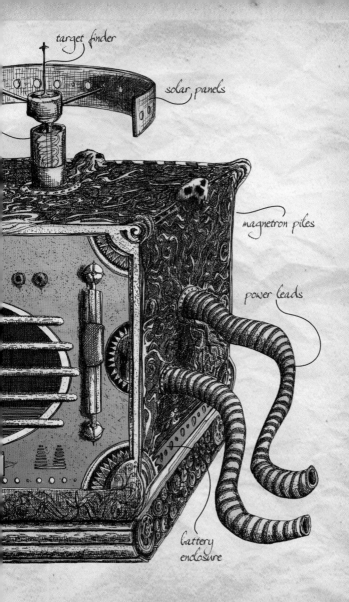

target finder

solar panels

magnetron piles

power leads

battery enclosure

SH/HLB/07/I897:
THE CORNISH DELIGHT PLOT
* * *

MISSION: to be a diabolical intrusion in the affairs
of men as ever, exploiting their foolish greed for
my pleasure. To wreak havoc while the weak seek
revenge. To fox and foil Holmes, to uproot him from
his sneering smugness. To take his life, or that of
the doctor who will not leave his side

My puppet Tregennis used the stolen African powder
to perfection and rattled Holmes. An earlier attempt
by another of my less experienced agents resulted
in his early descent into madness. Such is the life
of crime. His is being lived now in Helston with the
brothers. Holmes and the doctor nearly succumbed in
their effort to puncture my plot. So close! I could
have taken them both. I can see their corpses now,
their faces contorted, their eyes bulging from their
sockets, his drug-weakened brain gripped by a fatal
madness. And then the idiot Mortimer (was ever a name
so apt) was taken by Sterndale after the dolt vicar
sent word of his siblings' gratifyingly gruesome
fate. I was nearly undone, unmasked. Sherlock wants
no part in his punishment. Damn him to Hades. He may
not seek applause but I want my moment of glory.

NOTES: Holmes, exhausted by all my masterful
machinations and his psychotic need to unravel them
and outwit me, assisted me in my mission. His own
choice of relaxation is my private ally and this time
left him teetering on the precipice of a breakdown.
My desire was to push him rudely over that perilous
ledge into Podhu Bay, where sailors' brains are often
dashed on evil reefs.

Flower (harmless)

Leaf
(causes mild
hallucination when
taken as an infusion)

Root
(induces madness
when administered
in powdered form)

(Radix Pedis Diaboli)

"Gladstone"

"Tsar Nicholas"

"Florence Nightingale"

"Charles Darwin"

"Emmeline Pankhurst"

"Sitting Bull"

"Sherlock Holmes"

"Queen Victoria"

*he makes a deuced
attractive filly*

57

June 2, 1888

I selected Jemmy Sartoria by applying my usual meticulous precision. He was a man after my own heart and there was something of my younger self in him. Access to the first floor at 221b was no facile feat and to plant a bug in Holmes' meerschaum or violin (the affectations of the man!), no mean mission to give the young man, talented though he was. Sartoria was a smart choice in all senses of the word. Dressed as a gentleman, if somewhat on the dandy side of elegant, he could gain access to the rooms posing as a man of wealth and standing with a crime to resolve. Which he did to great effect, secreting the device in the pipe while distracting the famously observant detective with a tale that had more than an odour of Zaird Renee. Victory is sweet. It courses through me like a vintage wine after a fatal evening.

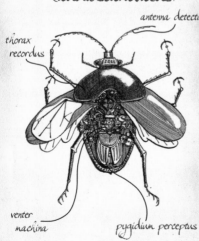

The listening bug
(audioscarabaeus)

antenna detecta

thorax
recordus

venter
machina

pygidium perceptus

POLICE
WANTED

MR JEMMY SARTORIA,
AKA *The Dandy Burglar*

Bit of an earnest fop, what?

SUBSTANTIAL REWARD OFFERED
FOR INFORMATION LEADING TO CAPTURE

April 1, 1888

I have undertaken to become a quick and confident exponent of the latest art of self-defence — Bartitsu. I am compelled to surprise my foes before they surprise me, there being a number of them, although just one upon whom my mind, and soon-to-be tutored muscles, must focus. It is imperative that I stay one step ahead of him, as the most dangerous man in London surely must. My goal is to upset the equilibrium of his body in tandem with his mind. I have enrolled in classes run by a moustached tutor, one Barton-Wright, held in a huge white-tiled gymnasium in the bowels of Soho. I shall master the art of Japanese wrestling and aim to be the most proficient stick fighter. Monsieur Vigny claims that La Canne will keep us safe in the gang-ravaged cesspool of London. The streets are indeed violent and thus satisfying. I shall enjoy tackling foul ruffians with nothing but my bicycle.

Umbrella and walking sticks should prove useful weapons to master. I relish the idea of inflicting pain on my enemy with the jab, thrust and downward cut. I shall master the kick and take firm hold of the various grips if it is the death of me. The value of the overcoat as weapon continues to flummox both me and, indeed, Moran, for whom there is no substitute for a bullet. Like Holmes he enjoys the intermittent firing of small arms, but usually outdoors, with a lucrative target in his sights.

Holmes' reputation as an accomplished boxer abounds and annoys in equal measure. Fleet of both foot and mind, it seems he is as dexterous with his limbs as with his brain cells. Damn him to hell, I shall be a better master of this Japanese art although its effects currently elude me. I have no plans to go home in a cart. And he cannot even spell the name correctly!

A SELF-DEFENCE CLINIC FOR GENTLEMEN

LEARN BARTITSU with E.W. BARTON-WRIGHT

LEARN HOW A MAN MAY DEFEND HIMSELF AGAINST ATTACK BY RUFFIANS AND ASSAILANTS USING A WALKING STICK OR UMBRELLA

PIGPENS

i.

i ⌐┘⊐∇□ <⊐⌐⊐⌐ ⌐⊏>

ii ⊐□⊐⊐< ∨⊐⌐>⊏ ⌐⌐⊐

iii ⊔⌐⌐⊐□⊐ □∨⌐⌐⊏ >□∨

iv ⊐⊏⌐⌐⌐ ⌐⌐><

v ⊐⊏⌐⌐> <⌐⌐

vi ⊐⊏⌐⊐□ *Tiger?!!*

vii ⌐<⊏⊐□ □⊐□□□
⌐⌐⌐∨ >

SHIFTED PIGPEN

i ⊐⌐⌐⌐⌐ ⊐⌐⌐⌐⌐

DANCING MEN

i

PIGPENS

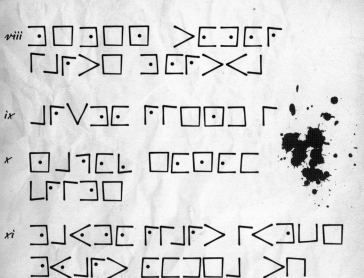

viii

ix

x

xi

ELDER FUTHARK

i ᛗᛟᚱᛁᚠᚱᛏᛁᚪᛗ

Bent the brain trying to work these out. Not my idea of a good time but see what you can do yourselves!!!

SH/HLB/05/I890:
THE BAKER STREET HORROR

***

MISSION: to assassinate Holmes by means of a deadly
poison. Tapanuli fever or black Formosa corruption

Sherlock Holmes is often to be found lurking around
Limehouse amd Rotherhithe, where the Chinese sailors
come in, so it will merely look like an unfortunate
accident. Moran has recruited a truly evil microbe
man, Culverton Smith of Sumatra, amateur of
disease, and I have contrived an innocent-looking
but fiendish device to administer said venom.
Culverton Smith has tried it out on his nephew,
Victor Savage, and it works perfectly. He took
almost four days of agonized suffering to die.

My plan was proceeding well when a sense of unease
came over me. A strange fever-like condition then
descended like a veil and began to work its tricks
upon me. I could not eat. I drifted in and out of
consciousness, flushed, a cold sweat upon my brow.
I did not feel myself. I was not myself. My grip on
reality was loosening as I rambled, speaking words
that were not mine. It was as if some foreign agent
had invaded my body and my reasoning. A poison
coursed in my veins. An alien sensation, a loss of
control. I could not eat and felt drained of life,
overwhelmed by insidious fatigue. I twitched and
jerked. My evil plans seemed to be slipping from my
grasp as my own grip on my consciousness loosened.

And then as the dark lid of this alien fever seemed
to lift so did a fresh horror descend. What I later

My innocent ivory weapon

sliding lid with concealed deadly spring

called the Baker Street horror. Seemingly free of
the illness, I was now victim to another, much worse
disease. My still fevered mind — for so it must have
been — imagined it was that of Holmes himself.
Hideous delusion and yet a chance, fleeting and
illusory as it might be, hallucinatory perhaps,
to be inside the mind of the detective I haunt and
taunt and shall defeat, to see how his drugged mind
operates; to glimpse the other side of the curtain,
where impotent light prevails. Where virtue holds
sway like a fool and justice struts and brags,
delivered by ruse. I saw Culverton Smith, my ally
in vice, captured by Holmes, but by cunning deceit,
a tool in my own armoury. Who is the victor here?

NOTES: Continue research into hypnotic substance
that allows me to enter H's mind safely, to browse
through its filing cabinet and peruse its drawers.

GHASTLY
MURDER
IN THE EAST-END.
DREADFUL MUTILATION OF A WOMAN.

Capture : Leather Apron

Another murder of a character even more diabolical than that perpetrated in Buck's Row, on Friday week, was discovered in the same neighbourhood, on Saturday morning. At about six o'clock a woman was found lying in a back yard at the foot of a passage leading to a lodging-house in a Old Brown's Lane, Spitalfields. The house is occupied by a Mrs. Richardson, who lets it out to lodgers, and the door which admits to this passage, at the foot of which lies the yard where the body was found, is always open for the convenience of lodgers. A lodger named Davis was going down to work at the time mentioned and found the woman lying on her back close to the flight of steps leading into the yard. Her throat was cut in a fearful manner. The woman's body had been completely ripped open, and the heart and other organs laying about the place, and portions of the entrails round the victim's neck. An excited crowd gathered in front of Mrs. Richardson's house and also round the mortuary in old Montague Street, whither the body was quickly conveyed. As the body lies in the rough coffin in which it has been placed in the mortuary —the same coffin in which the unfortunate Mrs. Nicholls was first placed—it presents a fearful sight. The body is that of a woman about 45 years of age. The height is exactly five feet. The complexion is fair, with wavy dark brown hair; the eyes are blue, and two lower teeth have been knocked out. The nose is rather large and prominent.

Foul play, Sir,
foul play!!

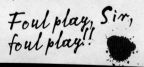

66

November 9, 1888

Jack gloats today as he stores his trophy on the shelf
of shame in some forgotten royal cellar. Light-hearted
Jack the Ripper, but not as light of heart as Mary.
He surpassed himself in the early hours. And so obvious!
Skinning your prey, disembowelling it, laying out organs
by the eviscerated carcass. Like writing your name on the
bloodied wall of the room. But the police feign blindness.
What more do the fools want? A calling card? If he
wrote his name in blood, it would be blue and Fortune
would render it invisible to any official eyes. The pack of
Inspectors, fed by the Establishment and answering their
hunting cry, doff their hats, bow their heads and lower
their eyes before royalty. Blue blood courses through his
veins, the arrogant cove, while red rivers run through the
slums of the East End. He will never be taken.

My name is on the lips of some in Whitechapel and
higher circles. It is whispered with awe and terror in
the highest and lowest of circles, instilling fear in fallen
women and impotent officials alike. Holmes must fear I
play a part in the orgy of organs and that brings me
some satisfaction. How easy my schemes would be if
I enjoyed the same protection as this gore-monger. What
great excesses of infamy would be within my reach! But
the rewards are not mine this time. His blue-blooded
hands are steeped in the red stuff yet remain unshackled.
I am bound by my Irish stock

Coin Press Prototype

Another genuine disaster!

SG/TASH/OI/I888:
A PRESSING MATTER

***

MISSION: to dupe the financiers, to duplicate their sycophantic royal currency and to double my fortune in order to create more mayhem and fund more experiments

When a man has mastered mathematics, it is time to turn to matters of a more material sort. The power of the equation thrills me: my criminal mind and knowledge of machinery delivers a concrete solution: counterfeit currency, simultaneous product and agent of sin. My press is a mirror of my soul, equipped to execute deceit, ruse and extortion, with the power of alchemy to turn fuller's earth to silver, just as I make evil of virtue and wreak havoc in high circles.

The press failed and the engineer Hatherley was lured by his own greed and my German minions to fix it, his predecessor having been a necessary sacrifice. But he suffered a very serious accident after smelling a rat buried in fuller's earth; the idiot woman helped him escape and he ran, thumbless, bleeding half-wit, to Holmes. BUT we outwitted the lauded detective. My agents escaped with their lives (of little interest to me) and the coins, box upon box of them.

NOTES: I struggle to decide which is sweeter: the thought of Holmes thwarted or my fortune set fair to expand so that the dark cloak I throw over this world can grow larger.

LAB NOTES: INVENTION OF MORIARTIUM
JUNE 1889

* * *

The creation of moriartium, an undetectable but highly effective poison, a colourless, odourless toxic compound that can be administered in a variety of forms, all to painful effect, and in carefully calculated strengths. There is no known antidote. MO_2 shall be my chemical signature.

It can be sniffed, inhaled, ingested, absorbed or even smoked (a minion will slip it into Holmes' pipe and rob him of his senses, identity and powers of detection for days while I wreak my havoc). It can be injected into the skin. When heated to a powdered form it can be put into food. It worked a treat on that stable lad in King's Pyland. If absorbed in a large enough dosage it administers a fast but painful death on its still conscious victim. Holmes may enjoy self-indulgent dilettante chemical investigations in the confines of his own home but my own experimentation is a clinical and precise laboratory affair.

Moriarty Sure-Fire Four-Barrel Hypodermic

The moriartium dispensing hyper syringe

NOTES: The consulting detective may believe he can determine the presence of haemoglobin with his bungled tests on acid-charred benches, but his knowledge of chemistry is far less profound than my own. He is no consulting chemist. I shall put him in his place with my secondary, minor poison $MO_{22}IB$.

Molecular formula for moriartium

Effect upon a large rat, male, when injected

Within 2 seconds: fainting attack
Within 3 seconds: convulsions
Within 5 seconds: organ failure
Within 6 seconds: paralysis
Within 10 seconds: death

Equal parts of:
1. opium
2. mercury
3. obscurantium
4. schizophrenium acid

SH/TVOF/1888:
OPERATION STOOL PIGEON

***

MISSION: to make money from the Scowrers, steeped
both in the spoils of American crimes and mines
and a deep seam of revenge upon their infidious
infiltrator, Birdy Edwards

It should have been a simple matter of eliminating
McMurdo, Birdy Edwards, now John Douglas, the
many-named, two-faced traitor, deceiver, fake
faker of coins, once I had cleverly located him
in his moated manor at Birlstone in England.
Only I could furnish the vengeful gang members
not hanged with instructions upon the manor's
whereabouts. Who else would have been able to
advise on the crucial timings of the drawbridge?
Even with the doltish, double informant Porlock's
pathetic attempt to give Holmes a tip-off. Why, oh
why, didn't Baldwin just pay me to wipe the former
Pinkerton detective from the face of the earth?
Instead of insisting on doing the job himself and
getting his face blown off with his own sawn-off
shotgun, thereby allowing Douglas, grand deceiver,
to add another fakery to his great armoury of deceit
and swop Baldwin's bloodied body for his own. Even
McGinty might have pulled it off had he not been
scaffolded by Birdy Edwards in Vermissa. How I
would have enjoyed tracking down a double-crosser
masquerading as an agent of the law and justice
and made a better job of it than any Scowrer, enemy
of God and man. But no, Holmes intervened, helped
by hapless Porlock and the hand of chance, and

Douglas was allowed to go free on a claim of self-defence. And what does Doyle know of my real nature, of my unsurpassed skills at my chosen career? He insults and misjudges me. I am no Napoleon-gone-wrong. I am the maligned master.

NOTES: I would not rest until justice was done and Birdy Edwards sent to a watery grave. Nobody escapes my retribution. I am a master criminal after all. Jonathan Wild was a mere precursor. Half a criminal. I am the full-blooded genuine article.

Without me he would be nothing!

But in calling Moriarty a criminal you are uttering libel in the eyes of the law – and there lie the glory and the wonder of it! The greatest schemer of all time, the organiser of every deviltry, the controlling brain of the underworld, a brain which might have made or marred the destiny of nations – that's the man! But so aloof is he from general suspicion, so immune from criticism, so admirable in his management and self-effacement, that for those very words that you have uttered he could hale you to a court and emerge with your year's pension as a solatium for his wounded character.

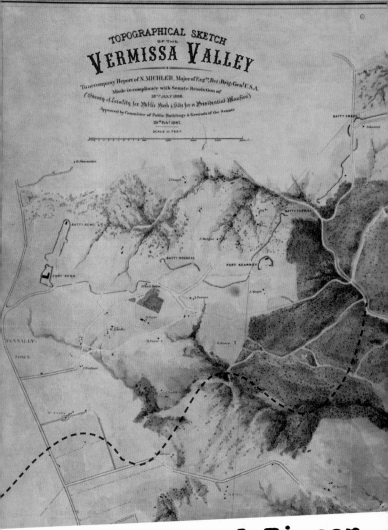

TOPOGRAPHICAL SKETCH
OF THE
VERMISSA VALLEY

To accompany Report of N. MICHLER, Major of Eng'rs Bvt. Brig. Gen'l U.S.A.

Made in compliance with Senate Resolution of
18th JULY 1866.

(Survey of Locality for Public Park & Site for a Presidential Mansion)

Approved by Committee of Public Buildings & Grounds of the Senate
20th Feb'y 1867.

SCALE 10 FEET.

BATTY SWEEN

D. Shoemaker

BATTY REWD

J. Nagee

BATTY VERMISSA

FORT REWD

BATTY ROSSELL

FORT KEARNEY

J. Hagee

School House

J. Palmer

TENNALLY-TOWN

J. Collette

H. Payne

R. Payne

J. Geary

C. Buckner

Wm A Coles

Operation Stool Pigeon

V.V.341

534 C2 13 127 36 3 14 17 21 41
DOUGLAS 109 293 5 37 BIRLSTONE
26 BIRLSTONE 9 127 171

Dear Mr Holmes

I will go no further in this matter. It is too dangerous — he suspects me. I can see that he suspects me. He came to me quite unexpectedly after I had actually addressed this envelope with the intention of sending you the key to the cipher. I was able to cover it up. If he had seen it, it would have gone hard with me. But I read suspicion in his eyes. Please burn the cipher message, which can now be of no use to you.

Fred Porlock

***

MISSION: to exploit the weakness of men for easy money and thereby make more of my own for my masterplan. To fix the lucrative Wessex Cup by putting Silver Blaze, out of the famous Isonomy, out of the running. Forcing Straker — how could I have known he was such an incompetent adulterer — to let Silver Blaze loose and damage the horse's tendon so that the famous favourite loses and I am victorious

Blackmailing Straker to drug the stable lad with a weak dosage of moriartium (incorrectly diagnosed later by the infernally curious Holmes as opium!) — it all seemed a simple plan that even the most incompetent of agents in my thrall could execute. But the puppet Straker collapsed at an early hurdle. I even instructed the fool on how to ensure his dog, silent with its master, would remain silent but able to alert him to unwanted visitors, during the releasing of the horse. The fool practised his cutting skills on sheep first! I was thwarted by idiocy but not by Holmes.

NOTES: If he were not dead I would not employ Straker again.

WESSEX CUP

50 sovs. each h ft with 1000 sovs. added, for four and five year olds. Second, £300. Third, £200. New course (one mile and five furlongs).

1. Mr. Heath Newton's **THE NEGRO**. RED CAP. CINNAMON JACKET.
2. Colonel Wardlaw's **PUGILIST**. PINK CAP. BLUE AND BLACK JACKET.
3. Lord Backwater's **DESBOROUGH**. YELLOW CAP AND SLEEVES.
4. Colonel Ross's **SILVER BLAZE**. BLACK CAP. RED JACKET.
5. Duke of Balmoral's **IRIS**. YELLOW AND BLACK STRIPES.
6. Lord Singleford's **RASPER**. PURPLE CAP. BLACK SLEEVES.

The Moriarty Dog Training Manual

1 To silence a dog, first teach it to speak. Either wait until it is barking and then reinforce its canine tendency by saying "speak" as it barks, or induce it to bark. I find that grimacing at a dog while looking deeply into its eyes often has the desired effect, then use the command. Repeat at least twice daily.

2 When your dog starts to bark when you say "speak", begin to train it to stop. Keep a pocket of boiled meat fragments. Ask the dog to bark. Then ask it to desist. "Stop!" uttered in a confident tone is as good a command as any. Run through the bark/stop routine several times a day, but reward only silence.

3 After another week use the "stop" command on its own, and employ two or three others to run through the same routine with the dog. Accompany with more meaty bribes; mesmerised by your largesse, the dog will soon forget any thought of barking.

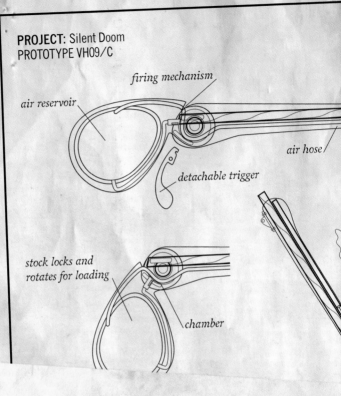

PROJECT: Silent Doom
PROTOTYPE VH09/C

air reservoir

firing mechanism

air hose

detachable trigger

*stock locks and
rotates for loading*

chamber

*Weapon of choice for hunting tigers
and humans (practised widely
on both species to great effect).*

AIR RIFLE REPORT BY: *Major Tim Sayer*

DESIGN: *Professor Moriarty*

CONSTRUCTION: *Von Herder, the famous blind German mechanic.*

PATENTED APPLICATION: *Rami Ramjets Oy,*

Finnish armaments factory

MECHANISM: *powered by a removable air reservoir*

to use expanding soft-nosed revolver bullets

OTHER FEATURES: *Barrel in form and guise of a cane*

REPORT: *powerful, noiseless, smokeless, highly effective*

RANGE: *approximately 50 yards*

lever is released from barrel to fill with air

4 5 6 7 8 9 10

Simple to use

Portable

My constant companion

Attached to it like a third arm or an extension of myself

SH/HLB/08/1914:
TO ARMS AND TO ARM
* * *

MISSION: to co-operate with the Kaiser, to shake
the English out of their comfortable somnolence and
to make the coast, indeed the skies, a less tranquil
place. To foment war in Europe in order to keep the
shareholders of Moriarty Defence Systems satisfied.
The Zeppelin project ia a greater drain on my
resources than anticipated

Treachery, deceit and smugness of the highest
order. Holmes at his most despicable, devious and
duplicitous. A hissing snake in the grass, weaving
his slippery, poisonous way across America and
Ireland, infiltrating my international network of
secret societies, hell bent on undoing the spies in
my pay. A slithery serpent of darkness masquerading
as a torchbearer of light, leading us into the
sunshine, or so he seems to imagine fondly. I think
not. The horizon looks satisfyingly dark to me.

Damn him from Buffalo to Berlin! How did he
penetrate my cleverly constructed plans to hand
over information to Germany? How did the buffoon
Von Bork, vain deluded German fool, fail to realise
that the bitter Irish American turncoat was neither
of those things. A man doing his best and worst to
betray his king and country and sell secrets to
their foes? Unlikely! Von Bork should have spent
less time perfecting his sporting and drinking
prowess as a cover and more time checking the true
identity of his agents. He underestimated the nature

of the English. His faculties were softened by his time in its devious countryside. Why did he not become suspicious at the way the other agents — James, Hollis, Steiner — were dropping like teeth from a fast-rotting jaw? How did he fail to grasp that Martha was no sleepy, self-absorbed housekeeper but part of Holmes' evil entourage. And Holmes himself — just who did the blaggard think he was? Altamont indeed! He should stick to his bees and leave me to pursue my crimes uninterrupted. I shall get level with him. If it takes me all my late lamented life!

NOTES: I must embark upon an expedition to foreign shores to find spies of a higher calibre. Holmes can stick to his bees. I have bigger missions.

"I shall get level with you, Altamont," he said, speaking with slow deliberation. "If it takes me all my life I shall get level with you!"

"The old sweet song," said Holmes. "How often have I heard it in days gone by. It was a favourite ditty of the late lamented Professor Moriarty. Colonel Sebastian Moran has also been known to warble it. And yet I live and keep bees upon the South Downs."

"Curse you, you double traitor!" cried the German, straining against his bonds and glaring murder from his furious eyes.

I do NOT warble it.
I mean it.

HMG/305/AFF/1914: OPERATION OSTRICH

* * *

MISSION: to execute a top secret order from a
European crowned head

God damn their tubercular eyes! Preserve us from
untrained zealots awash with nationalistic hubris.
Commissioned by the Kaiser (no need to keep it secret
any longer) I had conceived the perfect strategy.
It had taken months of meticulous planning,
liaison, smuggling in the air-guns in a shipment
of walking canes, setting up a plausible scapegoat,
infiltrating local press, etc. On June 28 my team
were primed and ready. Then just as our man Urban
had "accidentally" driven the royal car down
the wrong street, all hell broke lose. A scrawny,
mad-eyed little man started up, wildly firing
almost point blank at the Archduke. Moran amazed;
he has never seen a mark killed by sheer luck.
We had to abort our operation, but a couple of my
agents were so angry that they chased down the
miserable Princip and beat him mercilessly until
local officers took over. Apparently there were
seven of these rank amateurs. All they had were
pistols (which they couldn't fire), grenades (which
one of them lobbed into the wrong car) and cyanide
pills so enfeebled with age that they couldn't even
kill themselves in glorious martyrdom when caught.
No plan, no strategy, no intelligence. The whole
affair has been an insult to my professional pride.

NOTES: The Kaiser refuses to reimburse me (the job
is done, Herr Professor, nicht wahr?). I shall have
to remind him exactly who I am.

Of course, this ain't Holmes; it's one
of the few bits of paper I found that
don't refer to the blighter...
bad show, all the same

83

* * *

MISSION: to get my hands on Baskerville Hall using the rightful heir, son of Roger Baskerville, aka Stapleton, as my puppet after tracking him down in South America. A curse upon the thieving gentry

I have every right to take land and status just as those who now hold them did before me. Moriarty of Baskerville Hall would suit me well. I would do as other landed gentry do: exercise power over the poor and weak; benefit from the toil and labour of others without thanks or recompense; enjoy the fruits of their toil on the land and not share them equally. I have no need of a baronetcy, but its trappings should be mine.

Superstition and science — a satisfying mix. There is no more effective alliance than that of an unequalled intellect with an ability to exploit the weakness of men to bring about both justice and funds. It was a plan gifted from heaven and executed on a hellish foggy moor. The notion of a hellhound curse was scrawled in family history when Sir Hugo's throat was ripped by his own hounds after a kidnapped young wench died. What better gift could there be for a consultant in crime? I used it to terrify Sir Charles — his heart as weak as his spirit of generosity was pathetic (Laura Lyons did a fine job) — out of his wits, his hall and his life. The mission seemed accomplished, the £740,000 in its rightful place. All these magnificent machinations executed by using no

more than man's best friend, a mere dog, and an
ingenious application of luminescence combined
naturally with an enlightened, scientific, acute
criminal mind. Sometimes I think all I need is a
kennel of canines as accomplices. Their human
counterparts have so many failings and frailties.
And then I could hound H to the death.

But then the fools dug up their own rotting canker
in Canada — Sir Henry — and, drat him, Holmes was
alerted by the meddling Mortimer. Even Stapleton
seemed set to shoot us in the foot, stealing the wrong
boot to use as scent for the soft-hearted baronet and
unable to control his wife (how long did it take Holmes
to work that one out!) in her attempt to warn him of
the fate we had determined for him. He blabbed about
his past giving Holmes every opportunity to break
his cover and as any fool would, set a trap like a net
for a butterfly. Why oh why can't I find a puppet with
a committed constitution for crime? The Barrymores
provided a helping hand with their petty criminal,
Selden, who paid the ultimate price when he stole
Sir Henry's clothes. There is always wastage in
experiments. Idiots and weaklings, all.

NOTE I: Mission abandoned. But the Great Grimpen Mire
did not take me. Nor Stapleton.

NOTE 2: I must continue and perfect my research
into chemicals that can be used to commit much
greater crimes, taking my achievements to a higher
level. A weapon of great destruction must be my
goal. One with which I could hold not an estate,
not a county, but a country to ransom.

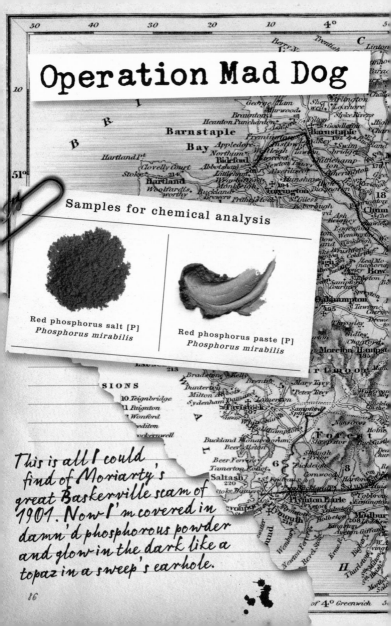

Operation Mad Dog

Samples for chemical analysis

Red phosphorus salt [P]
Phosphorus mirabilis

Red phosphorus paste [P]
Phosphorus mirabilis

This is all I could find of Moriarty's great Baskerville scam of 1901. Now I'm covered in damn'd phosphorous powder and glow in the dark like a topaz in a sweep's earhole.

Sir Henry Baskerville

Thorncombe

DORSETSHIRE

Membury
Dorset
Stockwood
worthy
Wellington
147
Axminster
Musbury
Lyme
143
Lyme Regis
Colyton
Seaton
River Yd
Combe

the moors

Tor Bay
Berry Hd
Brixham
Dittisham
Kingswear
Dartmouth Harbour
Stoke Fleming
Start Bay
Start Pt

DEVONSHIRE

SCALE

0   5   10   15   20 Miles

SOMERSET

CHANNEL

Dear Professor Moriarty

As your appointed administrator, a role I did not assume lightly, I feel compelled to write to you to advise in the most serious and graphic of terms that your mortality rates, as demonstrated by my Rose Diagram (enclosed), are disturbingly high and in need of immediate attention. The work of Monsieur Quetelet, a Belgian of high repute in this field whose figures I have studied closely and greatly admire, has made it clear that statistics are not merely numbers. They permit us as humans to take control of our own destiny. They demonstrate progress, progression, and reveal comparative success over successive years. Your own Rose Diagrams, Professor Moriarty – now that I have had time to look closely at them – confined as I am, are wanting in most regards, and I urge you to pay close heed and take the necessary action. I too took on the Establishment, albeit from an easier beginning than your own. In that we are similar. In all other affairs, we seem to be diverging in our efficiency at charting mortality.

Yours faithfully,

Florence Nightingale

January 8, 1886

Today I received a letter from F.N., castigating me about the disturbing pattern of statistics in my chosen sector, as revealed graphically in yet another of her blessed Rose Diagrams. She chastised me roundly for my "failings". I prefer to call them uneven successes. My own career path is pitted, no littered!, with the casualties and pitfalls introduced by lesser humanity. I am consistently wounded, sometimes almost mortally so, by the weakness of my minions. As a nurse she should be only too aware of such secondary factors and make allowances when administering my affairs.

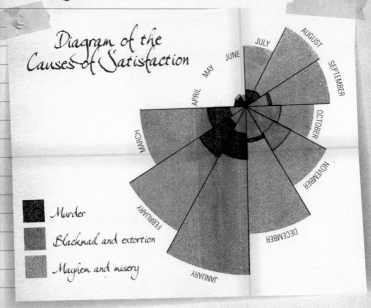

Diagram of the
Causes of Satisfaction

■ Murder

■ Blackmail and extortion

■ Mayhem and misery

MISSION: to lay my hands on one of the most precious public possessions

Recruiting Sir George Burnwell was not difficult. An aristocratic rake, imbued with unusual powers, particularly over the opposite sex, he was, like me, often low on funds and kept unusual hours, ripe meat for blackmail. He would easily find himself well placed to take from his corrupt milieu the things that rightfully belonged to mine. His seduction of the pathetic Mary H proved eminently useful when her uncle brought home the coronet from the bank for safekeeping. Much easier than recruiting a puppet at

Easily removed from setting

the office. Powerless to resist, she helped Burnwell make off with the jewels but the idiot Arthur tackled him before he could get them to me. However, fate was kind — Arthur landed himself in the frame and the brute force of Burnwell meant we had three coronets and were nearly home and dry when the deducting detective used his obsession with footprints to thwart us. Even I cannot account for snow!

NOTES: Another stroke of luck from Nature for Holmes. But Burnwell and Mary escaped capture so his victory is partial only. They will report to me soon or their necks are not safe. Meanwhile I shall work on my designs for a footprint eradicator.

The Moriarty All-in-One Footprint Fabricator & Eradicator (patent pending)

Note that with this versatile device one can:

* eradicate existing footprints
* lay down a false trail
* glide over the scene of the crime leaving no trace whatsoever.

It is a pedal-powered machine that makes little or no noise, so can be used nocturnally, with the addition of a dark lantern.

Devilish cunnin', what?

THE MILVERTON DEBACLE

* * *

MISSION: to squeeze ill-gotten gains from the aristocracy or to torture them until they fill my money-bags. To add horror to a horror-pocked universe, to bring dynamism to the dark forces in a world in which they swirl and eddy

Charles Milverton, already a promising sociopath, proved to be an excellent criminal under my sponsorship. He had become the prince of blackmailers, the second worst man in London. His methods were reliably cold and brutal, his demeanour and physique the same, and his results rewardingly consistent, if not consistently rewarding. There was always the odd high-born who failed to respond to sensible extortion, considering their class safe from it, above it, protected from it by their superiority - pah! Relieving them of their fortunes and their illusions of immunity through status and contacts was always a pleasure... I was on the whole proud of my protégé.

We had a number of concurrent cases, but after the foolish reluctance of the no longer Honourable Miss Miles to pay for our silence — how she must regret it — we decided that our next coffer-filling task would be the capsizing of the union of Lady Eva Brackwell and the Earl of Dovercourt. It was to be a very lucrative affair; Milverton had procured the compromising letters from a servant under his spell — a skill he had perfected under my tutelage, and one

And for me! I have them in my sights!

I suspect Holmes would brag of as his own. Holmes —
his hand is everywhere — then took it upon himself
to act as intermediary for the Brackwell woman and
tried to bargain with Milverton as if he were some
commonplace criminal.

After failing in his mission, Holmes stole our
modus operandi with surprising skill — the irony
would have been delicious had it not been so disastrous
— and assumed a campaign of seduction, deception
and blatant burglary to retrieve and then burn all
the papers, infiltrating Milverton's Hampstead
household with the apparent ease of a highly efficient
criminal. Milverton was shot by a female victim of
high repute seeking low, point-blank revenge — to my
slight relief as I suspected him of gypping me out of
my percentage. Holmes allowed the murderess to go
free. He believes he can play hide and seek with
justice too now does he? He seems too often to find his
sympathies lie with the villains but never with me.
A paradox if ever there were one. Is he judge, jury
and defendant? His attempts at the art of crime were
not without skill and his disguise as a plumber not
without success. On which side of the bench, the dark
line in the sand, does he stand?

NOTES: I must continue writing my manual of
blackmail. I seem to spend more time on the practice
of it than the theory but I am sure it would be
a bestseller and bring significant royalties in.
It might even bring significant royals down.

SH/TSOTF/1887:
OPERATION WOODEN LEG
✳ ✳ ✳

MISSION: to recover jewel haul stolen in Agra during the Indian Mutiny, ingeniously using Holmes as an unknowing catspaw

A complex, highly integrated plan that demanded attention to detail and split-second timing made all the more satisfying because after two mid-operation changes of plan (**volte faces** that only a criminal mastermind can successfully pull off) Holmes delivered me the haul without even knowing. Oh, the sweet irony. (Of course Doyle turned it into an incomprehensible rigmarole, but let it pass.)

Morstan was simplicity to gull, and I had the story out of him in the Langham grill (old India hands always want to share their imperial adventures) in a trice, shortly before he disappeared. Doyle has him sending for the daughter, but he did no such thing; one of the cousins, Mary, proved ideal when the plan came to pleasing fruition. It was just as easy to track Sholto down in his ludicrous Pondicherry Lodge and infiltrate "Benstone". Morbid greed made Sholto ingenious when it came to hiding what he had stolen, but I can play a long game.

Jonathan Small finally escaped and made his way to London where, annoyingly, the sight of him and his pegleg at the window was enough to frighten the odious Sholto to death, taking his secret with him. The insalubrious Sholto twins moled all over the garden to no avail, so I changed plan with the subtle cunning and finesse that marks my every

action. Dangling a pearl and a pretty face before
the easily besotted Watson instantly lured him, and
therefore the Baker Street narcissist, into the
game. Abducting them with their own consent from
the Lyceum was child's play; although it was tedious
beyond measure to listen to Holmes pretending to
geographical omniscience as I drove. My initial
strategem was for Holmes to find the treasure using
his "famous deductive method", and then we would
relieve him of it. Bart Sholto's death by dart
necessitated a second change of plan. I ordered
Jones to arrest the idiotic Thaddeus Sholto to
divert attention and furnished Small with a hollow
replica of his ersatz limb, into which he stuffed
the jewels. Dipping his toe in creasote to provide
an unmissable trail for Toby the scent hound to
follow, Small and Tonga escaped to lead Holmes
a merry dance along the river. When the Great
Numbskull finally caught up with them, and for
additional verisimilitude, I ordered Tonga to shoot
and miss. (Only I shall give Holmes his quietus.)
Small tossed the key to the decoy box in the Thames
and allowed himself to be gyved. Once in the solitude
of the cells, he emptied his leg into the custody of
Jones, and the jewels are now safely in our coffers.

NOTE I: It was vainglorious (but amusing) to allow
Jones to take Small to Baker Street and let him sit
there, a leg stuffed with gems, while the great
Pontificator pontificated. Must not get careless.

NOTE 2: Analyse the poison Tonga used on his thorns.

THE LANGHAM

DATE: August 30th 1889

Couverts: 3 on the account of
Mr Joseph Stoddart

Apéritifs – Amuse Gueules
Soupes – Consommé, Cucumber Soup,
   Mulligatawney
Poisson – Turbot à la Crème,
   Lobster Thermidor, Brill
Entrées – Broiled Mutton Chops,
   Beefsteak Pudding, Roast Rib
Desserts – Boiled Custard, Charlotte Russe,
   Whipped Syllabub
Savouries – Potted crayfish, Buttered shrimp,
   Anchovy toast
Fromages
Vins – Champagne Pol Roger, Bordeaux 78
   Château Lamothe-Guillard Sauternes, Port
Coffee & Digestifs

To dear Doy
Oscar X

THE SIGN OF THE FOUR,
Jonathan Small, Mahomet S
Abdullah Khan, Dost Akbar

Be at the third pillar from the left outside the Lyceum
Theatre tonight at seven o'clock. If you are distrustful,
bring two friends. You are a wronged woman, and
shall have justice. Do not bring police. If you do,
all will be in vain.

Your unknown friend

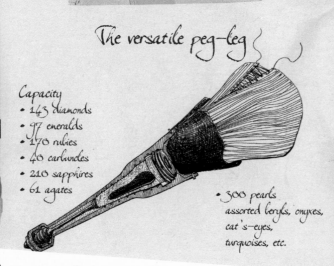

The versatile peg-leg

Capacity
- 143 diamonds
- 97 emeralds
- 170 rubies
- 40 carbuncles
- 210 sapphires
- 61 agates

- 300 pearls
  assorted beryls, onyxes,
  cat's-eyes,
  turquoises, etc.

Operation Wooden Leg

August 31, 1899

At Langham's (no one looks at a maitre d'); saw Jos.
Stoddart (from Zippincotts's), Doyle and Wilde dining together.
Doyle in evening dress looked like a walrus at the Ritz, but
Oscar took to him. It went to Doyle's head ("It was indeed a
golden evening for me!") and addled what little brain is there.
Not wanting to miss a commission, he turned my finely engineered
masterclass in criminal craft into an incomprehensible rigmarole.
He has the Nincompoop showing off like a mountebank,
bedazzling Watson (not difficult), spouting Goethe as if he
knew what it meant, downing McMurdo the prize fighter,
essaying insouciant wit which falls like bricks about the reader's
ears. And much shameless advertising of the Langham. Will find
out how much they paid him.

My Perfect Crime of the Century

I am enjoying an interlude from my usual business activities but my time will not be spent in indolence. I am preoccupied with the devising and designing of the perfect crime. Every man who pursues a career such as mine seeks to reach its very zenith. Every part of my brain is now engaged in this mission, which demands isolation and concentration. A one hundred percent solution of both. I have locked all doors to Butcher Street and am at home to no one. Moran knocks regularly upon the door, no doubt to demand his salary. Little does he know that it will multiply beyond all his reckoning should my plan succeed. Which it will.

I shall leave no trace of evidence. The means will be a mystery hidden deep within the belly of the ocean. The method will go to the starry heavens with me. The motive buried, drowned in a sea of uncertainty. That there is a crime at all shall remain unfathomable and unfathomed. I shall become wealthy beyond my sleepless dreams, the Croesus of the century. I shall sink the steamship Morituri.

The vessel will be laden with gold and jewels and precious, priceless artefacts, and its slumbering, complacent passengers robbed of all they own, not least their lives. My coffers will creak with the weight of the ship's cargo. Fate and Nature blamed, no hint for human hand behind the loss of life and loot will even be embarked upon. My name shall not go down — unlike the vessel — for I shall not be mentioned in any history books. Amid the wailing and wondering, the exclaiming and examining, I will be the nameless victor. Anonymity is not my friend, but for the perfect crime, I shall embrace it.

First, I shall recruit the most skilled and seaworthy of my Butcher Street Illiterati with the promise of voyage to America aboard the most luxurious of vessels. Their eyes will be as wide in acceptance as their gaping mouths in despair as they head to a watery grave, but only after they have steered the ship across the largest of icebergs, its position charted by me and imparted only to Moran. They will have secured all the treasure ready to disembark with it. I shall be aboard another unseen vessel following the _Morituri_ — I cannot risk the capsizing of my plan, confident although I am. As the ship sinks and the sabotaged lifeboats, too few in number — a precise calculation — spill their cargo into the freezing sea, Moran will make his way to my ship, bringing with him gold and jewels beyond measure and price, and using his trusty companion to ensure only he survives of my regulars. So much gained, so many Englishmen lost.

NOTES: Only a few details left to resolve. Moran must ensure the details of the luxurious _Morituri_ are sent to the greatest criminal minds in London. They won't be able to resist the lure of treasure, and where they go H will surely follow. I shall sink him if it proves the death of me.

September 16, 1885

I am essaying an experiment in the incitement of crowd violence; our operation is often in need of a baying mob, to protect escape routes, destroy evidence, distract witnesses and obstruct the plodding embodiment of the law. As a man of science, I am convinced that the common people, en masse, can be manipulated into a formidable weapon. Hours studying my formicarium indicate that with the strategic placement of one or two key goaders, crowds can be directed, amplified and dispersed at the direction of a higher intelligence with gratifying precision. My experiment took place in Ramsey, a wretched hamlet in the flatlands of north Essex, near Harwich. I chose it for its remoteness and the population (256), a statistically satisfying number.

I posited that it is possible to incite any crowd in any place by the use of a certain formula, based on ant communication. Only one or two initiator ants, charged with data, are necessary: if each of them pass the message on to four fellow ants, and they in turn pass on to four others — information (and misinformation) is spread with speed and efficiency. My disseminating agent was Jimmy Roastear (a lowly member of the organisation, but a sprinter of renown); to remove any bias, I fabricated a neutral grievance. The dull-witted populace of Ramsey is extremely fond of a grim confection of mangel-wurzel, apple peelings and sugarbeet which they call "jam", so Roastear spread the rumour of an imminent shortage of this vile, unpalatable conserve. The entire village was on his heels

The Echo

17th September, 1885

RAMSEY JAM RIOT

OUR CORRESPONDENT

Spontaneous outrage swept the village of Ramsey yesterday when the inhabitants learned that a shortage of local jam was imminent. One man was robbed of his life and several more sustained severe scythe wounds during the disturbance which lasted into the night when firebrands were lit, and the burning ricks could be seen from as far away as Mistley.

brandishing pitchforks and flensing knives within ten minutes, murdering the messenger being a basic instinct of mobs everywhere. I calculate that this could be done in half the time using a London crowd, on a more complex urban grid.

The experiment yielded useful lessons: the strategic use of crossroads, emergency corralling and how to stop a crowd in full spate simply by throwing small coins at their feet. Tomorrow I shall write it up in full in the workbook, including the algorithm that distils crowd control into a simple formula; it is too dangerous to confide to a diary.

No sign of the bally thing.

THE BLACK PEARL CONSPIRACY

✱ ✱ ✱

MISSION: to restore the black pearl of the Borgias to its rightful owner. My good self

It had my name written all over it and should have been mine from the start but — sentimental fool — I agreed to collaborate with my cousin Giacomo and his mafia network on this mission. Organised criminals they are not, family or no. One of their London-based agents — a capable enough operative under cover at the Dacre Hotel — stole the priceless pearl from the Prince of Colonna as planned, but the arranged handover to her brother Pietro was intercepted by a duplicitous, low-level, hideous, homicidal operator who lurked under the name of Beppo. Pearls before swine indeed! The jewel never reached the maid's brother Pietro, and professional relations with Giacomo were as chilled as a Sicilian winter. Beppo, violent, deluded fool, thought he could dupe Moriarty AND the Mafia and keep the pearl as a pension. We tried to get to him at his workplace, Gelder and Co., but the underfed ragamuffin in my meagre pay proved too weak for the brute. It was only on Beppo's release from prison a year later that we sniffed out that he had hidden the Borgia pearl in a plaster cast of Napoleon. Pietro was persuaded by my more muscle-bound minions that tracking Beppo on his hunt for the one bust that housed the Borgia pearl was good for his future, but it was cut short anyway when the brute Beppo slashed Pietro's throat during one of the searches. The mission, like the

Napoleons, was in shreds. Then, to make it worse,
Holmes got wind of it via Lestrade and tried to piece
it all together. Smug, obsessive solver of puzzles,
he got to Beppo before we did, trapped the brutal
Napoleon buster AND kept the pearl.

NOTES: Mission aborted. Giacomo owes me.

HARDING BROS.
ART & ARTEFACTS

*High Street Kensington
London S.W.*

DATE: *February 3, 1899*

TO: *Mr Sandeford, Lower Grove Road,
Reading, Berkshire*

FOR: *One plaster bust of Napoleon
after Devine*

Amount : 15 shillings

*Received With
Thanks*

PJM/SCJ/03/1901:
OPERATION X

* * *

MISSION: to perform the ultimate act of robbery
— to appropriate by stealth the crown and regalia of
England and ransom it back to an ungrateful nation

An undertaking as audacious as this demands the
controlling touch of a man of cosmic vision, courage,
daring, extraordinary nerve, mighty intelligence
and forensic grasp of detail: in short a Napoleon
of crime, a being whose grasp exceeds that of mere
mortals, especially that of the self-deluded Holmes.

I will inflict a blow upon the establishment that
will be felt throughout generations. Holmes may preen
himself on his bourgeois emerald pin (an insignificant
crumb dropped from the royal table into the maw of
a lickspittle lackey), whereas I shall have jewels
of such power in my possession that could, used
judiciously, bring about the downfall of empires.

Everything is in place. The perfect replicas I
commissioned from the finest forgers in Europe are
locked away in a secret vault. I would not be so devoid
of wit as to keep the details of this bold enterprise
where anyone may read them; spies are everywhere.
I shall strike at no known date or hour, and none
shall know whether the very symbol of British power
is truly sovereign, or worthless fakery. Ha!

NOTES: Moran to silence replica makers.

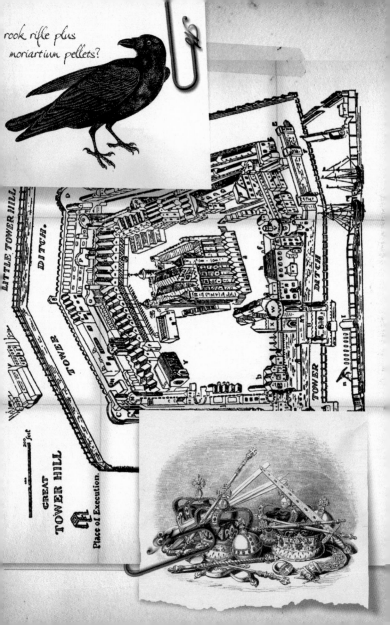

rook rifle plus
moriartium pellets?

LITTLE TOWER HILL

DITCH.

TOWER

TOWER

DITCH

200 feet

GREAT
TOWER HILL

Place of Execution.

* * *

MISSION: to make disappear damage caused by a
botched endeavour on the part of Her Majesty's
government (inflicting humiliation on Holmes was
to be a bonus)

Holmes' brother, Mycroft, the self-styled embodiment
of Her Majesty's Government, occasionally calls on
my services when his masters do not want their hands
sullied. We meet at the Diogenes Club, founded by him,
and funded by HMG specifically for this purpose. The
quid pro quo is a free rein to pursue my own private
enterprises, unhindered by tedious bureaucracy.

The Kratides twins were Greek spies; on a secret
mission to London, Sophy Kratides was under orders
to inveigle herself into the affections of Mycroft's
agent Harold Latimer; he was ordered to reciprocate.
Apparently she fell in love with him and defected,
offering official secrets in return for asylum.
These were useless without the cipher key, known
only to her brother Paul. She lured him to London,
where he was kidnapped and tortured by Latimer
and his psychopathic henchman Wilson Kemp (why
Mycroft insists on such episcopal **noms-de-guerre**
eludes me). He would not talk. Distrusting Sophy,
Mycroft arranged for his harmless neighbour,
Melas, a Greek interpreter, to be escorted with
cudgels to the safe house. Paul, obviously one of
those pointlessly heroic fellows, stuck to his cover
story about property, presumably to spare Melas.

Impasse. Mycroft suggested to Melas that he consult Sherlock (Mycroft can be extremely spiteful) and sure enough, the Baker Street Blunderer was soon thundering about all over south London (how he loves those dreary suburbs — inexplicable), creating a magnificent diversion.

Mycroft had no qualms about sending Melas into the lion's den once more, which was the signal for my agent Davenport to warn them that Sherlock, Watson and Lestrade were on their way, like the cavalry — late, loud and useless. Kratides must have finally broken, and they had left him for dead, but milksop Watson brought Melas around, creating further administrative complications. Latimer, Kemp and the girl had gone, taking their lucrative secrets. I alerted our agents in Europe and some months later, the men were found dead in Budapest. Holmes, the romantic naïf, opined that Sophy had done it to avenge her brother (he had believed completely the folderol about Sophy's property) and so looks foolish; and I have in my vault some sensitive information that the Greek government will pay me well to have back.

NOTE: Exploit Mycroft's morbid indolence.

Diogenes Club

MYCROFT HOLMES
Co-Founder

March 7, 1891

These quarterly meetings are always tedious beyond
comprehension. The official minutes are filed in our vault
at the laboratory, but I find it soothing to vent my spleen
in the privacy of my diary. My operation has a board
of trustees (for legal reasons I do not propose to give
those few members of the establishment not in my pay
any reason to swoop), but it comes at a high price. It
was a fractious meeting, as usual; it is my expertise,
my intelligence, my daring strategies that fill the coffers;
they receive a generous dividend in exchange for their
signatures, yet all they can do is bicker. And they all
talk at once, despite Mrs Hudson's jaw-locking way
with a macaroon. Oat Jay Rimmers evangelises fibre, Aimer
Tramjoys, the Walloon textile magnate, and Joris Maymert,
the cocoa heir, gibber to each other in Flemish, a language
no civilised being should own to knowing; and you would
think that Sir Tommy Aarje, the Dutch munitions king,
would be grateful for his knighthood (it took a deal of
arranging), but there he is nitpicking at the bottom line like
a grocer's clerk. At least Jim Roastermay, our Queensland
representative, holds his tongue. Only Mortmaier and
Ramjay Moister, the Indian-Bavarian steel baron, share
my vision and understand the sheer scale of my plans.

I had to crack the whip; they are here to report to me,
not gainsay my commands, and I am damned if I am
going to explain my every expenditure. Moran is always in

the corner and it is almost worth the colossal stipend I
pay him just to watch them quail when he starts fingering
his stick. We agreed a budget finally, but I refuse to
countenance any notion of bonuses.

ROYAL FLUSH

* * *

MISSION: to find and extract the ancient crown of England last worn by Charles I from the grounds of Hurlstone House under the noses of the Musgraves

This was a long game. Our agent Brunton, insinuated himself as butler to the Musgraves at Hurlstone some 20 years ago; I did not think he would last; not many butlers speak several languages and play nearly every musical instrument, but the Musgraves were too busy banging away at pheasants to wonder why. They were too dense even to understand the significance of their own ritual, although I of course was not. Then, on the brink of a solution, Brunton disappeared. I suspected a double cross.

Mistrusting my own agents, I thought of manipulating Holmes; he is addicted to puzzles, and I knew he could not resist the aristocratic nincompoop and old college colleague Reginald Musgrave, the oleaginous sycophant. Holmes worked it out pretty quickly (it was straightforward); Brunton's body was found in the cellar, but no sign of the treasure. Rachel Howells, one of Brunton's scorned women, had stuffed him in the oubliette and thrown the treasure in the lake and run away; Musgrave the Dim had dragged it out, but thought it just a mass of old rusted metal and dull-coloured glass. The gentry have no appreciation of beauty or history. Operation abandoned, much to my chagrin and displeasure.

NOTE: Discourage dalliances among agents.

"Whose was it?"
"His who is gone."
"Who shall have it?"
"He who will come."
"What was the month?"
"The sixth from the first."
"Where was the sun?"
"Over the oak."
"Where was the shadow?"
"Under the elm."
"How was it stepped?"
"North by ten and by ten, east by five and by five, south by two and by two, west by one and by one, and so under."
"What shall we give for it?"
"All that is ours."
"Why should we give it?"
"For the sake of the trust."

I say, Holmes couldn't see the wood for the trees, what!!!

Elm   Oak

111

The Magnolia Belle,
Mississippi, August 10, 1886

On my way to a tiresome meeting with the New Orleans branch, led by Jacques (James?) Moriarty; there was something seriously amiss with the last consignment of voodoo paraphernalia); sliding along the oily waters of the great Mississippi is a not unpleasant sensation and relatively silent; I was noting down how the tacit propulsion worked, for possible use on our own boats — river piracy is a lucrative area — when I was accosted by a refined southern gentleman, shuffling a pack of cards in one hand. "Good morning sir, allow me to introduce myself, Easy Jim Mortar of New Orleans at your service. I wonder if you would care to play a little leisurely poker with me and my colleagues to while away the hours?" I deduced that my accent signalled that I was an easy mark. Yet I had some hours to pass, so I acceded. Mr Mortar regaled me with tales of his youth in the Civil War and how things had been so much more gracious in the antebellum days and how he missed his family mansion, burnt down at the Battle of Port Hudson.

Winning at cards is merely a matter of close observation, numeracy and perfect recall. When I had taken $15,000 and noticed, via the huge mirror in the grand salon wall, that Mr Mortar was preparing to insinuate marked cards into the deck, albeit dextrously — only someone as eagle-eyed as myself would have seen it — I withdrew.

I considered having him shot,
but thought better of it; he
is an excellent craftsman, a
rare combination of charm,
brains and a total freedom
from moral discernment. I
shall make him an offer he
will be unable to refuse.

Easy Jim took
me for 500
sovs back in
'82, blast him!

THE CARFAX INHERITANCE

* * *

MISSION: to access Lady Frances Carfax's abundant
inheritance from which her gender denies her

My agent Philip Green, once an ardent admirer of Lady
Carfax, had been spurned by her family for his lack of
money. Learning that his paramour could be a woman of
substance if married, I furnished him with money and
a plausible background in South Africa and urged him
to woo her again, with the intention of blackmailing
him into signing the money over to me after the event.
He is a passionate dolt and easily led. The operation
was compromised when loathsome Australian confidence
trickster Henry Peters scented money and, playing Dr
Schlessinger the unworldly missionary, accosted the
lady in Switzerland and lured her into his clutches.

It was imperative to remove Peters without harming the
Green operation and Watson was surprisingly good at
persuading Holmes to step in. The plan was for Holmes
to find them using Green (at my orders); the Australians
were trying to pawn her jewellery, the small-minded
amateurs. She was sitting on a theoretical fortune and
they could not even find a decent fence. Holmes finally
worked out Schlessinger's signature coffin dodge and
Watson, amazingly, revived her. The ninny delivered
her to Green and Peters is on the run. A successful
result for us, made even better by the sight of Holmes
wringing his hands in the conviction that he failed.

NOTES: Investigate Lestrade. Why did he delay the
warrant, against my orders?

DESIGN PREPARED FOR
DR SCHLESSINGER by
STIMSON & CO

A modification of our very popular "Requiescat" model, this casket features veneer clad pine, solid brass fitments and furniture, double depth ivory slub silk lining and is 1 ft (12 ins) deeper than standard to accommodate a more than usually robust deceased.

406 KENSINGTON ROAD
LONDON SW

STIMSON & CO
UNDERTAKERS
Et in Arcadia Ego

DATE: *May 6, 1901*
FOR: *The interment of Mrs Rose*

	£	S	D
Laying out	3	0	0
Pallbearers	5	5	0
Four Horse hearse	15	0	0
Mutes	2	0	0
Gravediggers		2	6
Coffin: custom made	8	12	6
to bereaved's specifications			
Full amount due	34	0	0

handles lower than standard for more efficient weight distribution

THE MORIARTY CO-AXIAL HEIGHT:
VILLAINY CALCULATOR

Let H be height and V be villainy

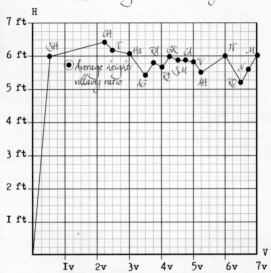

THE MORIARTY HEIGHT/VILLAINY CORRELATION

✱ ✱ ✱

With the help of Miss Nightingale, I have drawn
together a graph correlating the heights of various
men of triumphant villainous history with whom I
can compare myself; it has long vexed me that there
appears to be an opinion that arch criminals and
those perceived to be powerfully villainous are
always restricted of stature. As I myself am almost
6 ft tall, I perceive this as a slur on my capacity.
I opine that this calumny is, if not a statistical
anomaly, a species of propaganda; it makes the
forces of the law feel safer to make criminal
masterminds look small, whereas it is of course
the size of the brain that matters not the body
that carries it.

OBSERVATIONS

* Charlemagne was taller than self, but less
  villainous
* Robespierre was shorter than self and slightly
  less villainous
* Napoleon was shorter than self, yet almost
  equi-villanous
* Holmes is as tall as self, yet markedly less
  villainous

CONCLUSION: Height and villainy have no
correlation.

I ain't that short!!

COROLLARY: Tall people can be arch criminals.

* * *

MISSION: to have my revenge on Jephro Rucastle, who has wronged me and transgressed the rules of the organisation; to use the chance to watch Holmes clamber through some entertaining hoops

Some ten years ago, Mr Jephro Rucastle, the overfed upstart, chose to cross me in a matter of an Australian Bauxite mine share issue. Although I have rectified the situation financially and thus rendered him so penurious that he has had to resort to imprisoning his own daughter for fear she marry and her husband demand the inheritance from her mother (interest from which Rucastle uses to support himself, his dull second wife and their odious offspring), that is not enough for me. He must feel my displeasure in his bowels.

Irene as Violet Hunter looked very well in her chestnut wig. Watson, the unmitigated dimwit, did not recognise her when she visited Baker Street. Despite her unwomanly ambition, she is an excellent actress, and delivered the farrago of utter balderdash we had contrived as a lure to Holmes with composure and aplomb (so Watson reported when he eventually realised who she was). Holmes instantly smitten, and, as planned, intrigued by the serpentine eccentricity of her story.

Soon he was galumphing down to Winchester at "Violet's" summons; this was issued as soon as our agent Mrs Toller had allowed Mr Fowler, the frustrated fiancé, into the house to rescue Miss Alice (I could have put my hands on the inheritance, but it was not large enough to bother with). With Toller inebriate, and the mastiff Carlo starving and ready to be let loose, it only needed Holmes to be thundering around Copper Beeches to outrage Rucastle (sent home by anonymous message). At Violet's command, Mrs Toller let loose the hound, who instantly attacked Rucastle (she had impregnated his trousers with meat extract while pressing them). Watson shot the dog dead, neatly removing any evidence and now Rucastle is a life-long invalid trapped in a domestic hell with his unspeakably boring family and servants. I will not be crossed.

NOTE I: Watson reports that Holmes is not actually smitten with Violet Hunter, but the enigma she presented; the man is a fool. Irene extremely put out by his indifference, which is very vexing for all in her vicinity.

NOTE 2: Replace Carlo; he was out of the hound of the Baskervilles by Rotherhithe Ruby, one of Sherman's stable of stolen pedigrees.

October 22, 1898

Dr Doyle is a cloth-eared philistine. I weary of the lack of acknowledgement; the blundering dolt of his preposterously popular tales would be nothing without me. My cogent arguments that the work would be far more effective were I to be cast as the protagonist goes unheeded. I am by far the superior brain, my personality is shot through with subtlety and intrigue, interweaving strands of dark and darker. Pearls before swine. Then I discovered that Doyle's sister Constance was marrying Willie Hornung. He is a man of the world, a decent hack — at least better than Doyle; let him write about me — he would find overnight fame and have the advantage of his sanctimonious relative by marriage. I outlined my ideas to him, suggested how he might contrive a species of literary mirror to Doyle's penny dreadful ramblings. Terms were agreed.

Perfidy! I have before me a copy of Cassell's Magazine, and what, but what, do I read within? A yarn by Hornung, not, as agreed adumbrating the adventures of a criminal mastermind, but a farcical gallimaufry about a gentleman thief called Raffles and his lap dog "Bunny" Manders? I offer him a Napoleon of crime and he contents himself with a willow-wielding thug with a talent for disguise, a travesty of our agreement; I am traduced; I will think long and hard about appropriate revenge.

Gentleman thief?
I think not.

THE M CLASS MORIARTY
IMPROVED HANSOM CAB

The M class is based on a standard hansom chassis, with reinforced axle and double-skin horsehair stuffed bodywork. Refinements include a brace of wheel-mounted Barber & Janes .44 revolvers, a miniaturised retractable Moseley-Garrard 30mm cannon, a cutting device from Blades of Sheffield and an Ansell prismatic periscope. All are controlled from a roof-mounted console in front of the driver, with an override switch within the cab.

Roll down steel apron

Ejector seat mechanism

Whirling blades

Folded leather tarpaulin

Oil reservoir (can be released to form slick or fuels smoke pipe)

Compartments in wheel that open to dispense small stones/caltraps/nails

Never got to drive the thing, damn shame

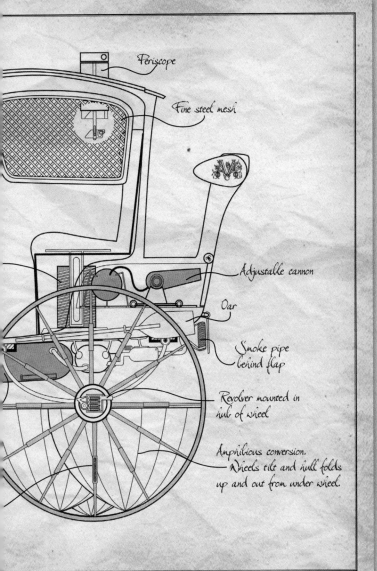

Periscope

Fine steel mesh

Adjustable cannon

Oar

Smoke pipe
behind flap

Revolver mounted in
hub of wheel

Amphibious conversion.
Wheels tilt and hull folds
up and out from under wheel

JJM/FE/OOI/I893:
OPERATION HOT AIR

✳ ✳ ✳

MISSION: to acquire the Fabergé egg in the possession of émigré Count and Countess Curnonsky to add to my collection; for too long there has been a gap, and I wish to gaze on perfection only

The team numbered notorious balloonist and jewel-thief Jean-Jacques Montgonflier (who was after the Curnonsky emerald and diamond parure, tawdry baubles in my eyes), his maître de ballon Etienne Paul, their trained capucin Dupin and Petra Mostvoda, the cross-dressing cat burglar. The Curnonskys were guests at the Le Touquet residence of financier Jay S Mortmaier and had brought with them all their jewellery and the exquisite ovoid, only the possession of which would quench my lust.

Mostvoda, guised as a young waiter, cracked the safe, removed the jewellery and my precious egg, replaced them with near perfect paste replicas, wrapped the originals in an oiled silk bag and threw them out of the window where they were caught by Dupin waiting in the trees. I feared for my egg, but the capucin is as deft-fingered as he is nimble, and within minutes was running up the ropes of the balloon waiting on the nearby strand. Paul loosed us from the surly bonds of earth and we were away. I gazed enraptured at my beautiful egg gleaming enigmatically in the white starlight, calm of mind, all passion spent.

NOTES: Perfect execution, no revision necessary.

M. Montgonfliers Aerial Conveyance, Le Pegasus

The cream of the jest is that Mr I-see-all Holmes was employed to prevent just such a robbery and the dunderhead missed it completely!

Mostvoda even served him a drink before she slipped away into the night.

July 7, 1896

!!!!

A particularly vexatious and dyspeptic day; the monthly strategy meeting with my closest operatives and minions always is: Moran sits like a suet pudding, but has the virtue of silence; Irene, I fear, is starting to believe that she is actually an operatic diva and agitates for her Byzantine blackmailing schemes to be implemented; Mrs Hudson can do nothing with her, but what mother can tame a wilful daughter?

I run these meetings on principles derived from my formicarium: we are a cellular organisation with information passed on only to those who need to know it. When endangered, any cell can be cauterized, so that the operation remains uncompromised. Even I would have to immolate myself should I be apprehended, a circumstance that I do not anticipate. Operatives come and go individually to report and receive orders (the Butcher Street Illiterati always last, because the stench is overwhelming). Today Shinwell Johnson, our double agent (Holmes, the condescending dunce, thinks he is loyal because he doffs his cap) came up with some useful snippets that could advance the Guilful conspiracy (see workfile SJ 7/96). Watson late, as usual; suspect the weak-willed, skirt-chaser has gone over to Holmes, but no matter, his naïve babblings tell me all I need to know, and it is almost enjoyable feeding him disinformation to pass on to Doyle. Nothing new from the Yard, but Sherman the taxidermist and the odorous Toby brought gratifying news from the docks.

July 10, 1896

I find I am concentrating more on goading Holmes these days, and leave the bulk of the non-Holmes missions to my brother Colonel James Moriarty; I note with slight amusement that many dull minds assume that he holds a military rank, but his name, Colonel, is merely a fancy of my father's to differentiate him from me. He lacks my panoptic vision, but can be relied on to follow my orders exactly, and is a master of logistics, and with no little cunning. He has convinced Baker Street's Great Mind that he is a negligible railway employee, a "stationmaster in the West country". What better cover for the marshaller of our arachnid communications system? Once again, Holmes is revealed to be a gullible halfwit, insensitive to the obvious.

August 1, 1896

A fruitful day in the laboratory. I have of course meticulously noted the results in the laboratory journal, but this particular experiment was very pleasing in its elegance. By subjecting radium to gentle pressure and applying a trick I have devised to a water boiler, I have contrived to create a jet of steam which is inexhaustible. This has never been achieved before, but on considering the results anew, I think it behoves me to keep them from public scrutiny to protect my mine share investments.

MISSION: to enjoy the rewards of others' crimes

It began in the Antipodes. Few continents escape
the net cast by my dark web of crime. Jack McCarthy
had been my man for many years. I first knew him in
Australia as a wagon driver not averse to bribery
in return for forged miners' rights documents. I
found him on his uppers back in London and upon
hearing his tale of near death during a robbery
in the gold fields it did not take long to discover
which highwayman he had escaped. My spies tracked
the so-called reformed murderer down in Boscombe
Valley with some ease.

Turner, ex robber-cum-landowner with a Ballarat
booty, was leading a virtuous life in England. A man
cannot ever be wholly free of crime, however hard
he turns his face to it or whatever his surname!
Crime is written in ink that stains the very soul.
It may be lightened but never washed clean. Under
my instruction, McCarthy began a campaign of
regular extortion using the threat of exposure of
the man's past as his constant watchword. I kept
my coffers topped up with a fair percentage of
Turner's property, land and money, a satisfying
arrangement, with McCarthy taking a small share.
But he wanted every last drop, even for Turner's
daughter to marry his own son. My henchmen could
not halt his greed even with our customary methods
but for Turner it was a demand too far and he
duped, trapped and killed McCarthy, whose own

son was then arrested for the crime. Holmes the meddler was called to bring justice — irony of ironies — using Fortune's hand and his maniacal obsession with cigar ash identification to acquit the son. Turner and his funds were taken from my grasp by death.

NOTES: Another stream of income called to a premature halt. Felled by Fate's tricks again. Not by the helpless worm of a detective...

This one should fool Holmes next time.

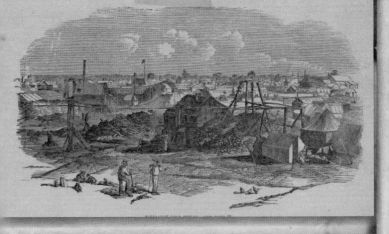

***

MISSION: to retrieve from the cellar of I56 Little Ryder Street, W. the counterfeit press and £I50,000 in forged Bank of England notes stored with it by our deceased master forger Rodger Prescott

Five years ago, Prescott, whose notes would pass anywhere, was pointlessly shot dead in a game of cards by another of our agents, James Winter, alias "Killer" Evans. Americans! This ruined several of our operations; Winter was left to rot in jail (although spared the noose), on the proviso he would get back the press and the bank notes on his release.

Although murderous, Winter had some nous, and set up the Mysterious Inheritance trick on the eccentric ancient who now lived in the premises, who had by great good luck a very unusual name, Garrideb. Posing as a John Garrideb, Winter winkled the reclusive buffoon out of the house (sending him to Birmingham after a fictional third Garrideb) while he cleared the cellar. Unfortunately, the real Garrideb got Holmes involved, so Winter had to improvise. Watson got shot (his reward for not throwing Holmes off the scent) but Winter was overpowered; the press and the money went back to the Yard, into the safe hands of Lestrade, so disaster was averted. Winter went back to jail, the incompetent hot-head.

NOTE: Do something about Watson.

HOWARD GARRIDEB

CONSTRUCTOR OF AGRICULTURAL MACHINERY

BINDERS, reapers, steam and hand plows, drills, harrows
FARMERS' carts buckboards and all other appliances
ESTIMATES for Artesian Wells

APPLY Grosvenor Buildings Aston

BANK OF ENGLAND

Chief Cashier

Promise to pay

the Sum of

For th

1845 Jan.t 28 L

He is a man of good birth and excellent education, endowed by nature with a phenomenal mathematical faculty. At the age of twenty-one he wrote *A Treatise on the Binomial Theorem,* which has had a European vogue. On the strength of it he won the mathematical chair at one of our smaller universities, and had, to all appearances, a most brilliant career before him.

December 5, 1893

I have just received advanced copies of Doyle's account of the Reichenbach Falls Incident. Usual Holmes—centric windbaggery, full of the Sage of Baker Street puffing on about how superior he is. I had to make three clumsy and obvious attempts on Holmes' life, then go chasing ostentatiously about the southern counties in a private train "looking for" H & W to get any attention; short of advertising my intentions in The Times, I could do no more. However, I was sanguine, I believed that I had finally got it through Doyle's thick head that a supervillain needs a bit of character, and that I deserve as much time on the page as Holmes gets, just to keep the readers interested. There's only so much you can do with a violin and a Persian slipper; I am much more evilly fascinating.

   And what do I find when I finally read "The Adventure of the Final Problem"? (Doyle never mastered the art of the snappy title.) Mentioned I may be, but in such an erroneous and patronising manner that it makes a mockery.

I was 18, not 21, when I wrote my Treatise; granted Binomial Theorem is pretty schoolboy stuff, but I know that Holmes wouldn't recognise Pascal's Triangle if he fell over it on one of his cocaine-induced wanderings. "One of our smaller universities." Tchah! This from the man who scraped a chemistry third from somewhere so obscure he never mentions it. I tried to calm myself, remember that I had in fact killed the blighter (although the scientist within nags for harder evidence than just a scrap of tweed ulster). I knew I should focus my mental energies on the Grand Unifying World Domination Scheme, but then I stumbled on the passage below. My extraordinary mental powers barely touched on, and everything, all my dark genius and devilish grasp of detail, my years of focused dedication to my cause, dismissed as an "inherited criminal strain". Pathetic. No scientific backing cited — Doyle can barely remember how many brothers I have, so is in no position to pontificate about genetic inheritance.

But the man had hereditary tendencies of the most diabolical kind. A criminal strain ran in his blood, which, instead of being modified, was increased and rendered infinitely more dangerous by his extraordinary mental powers. Dark rumours gathered round him in the University town, and eventually he was compelled to resign his chair and come down to London.

27

Who does he think he is?

133

FAMOUS SLEU

MYSTERY STR

Death of celebrated detective shocks the civilized world

POLICE REPORT IN FULL

Can Sherlock Holmes really be dead?
As the world struggled to comprehend the enormity of what has happened, police from Switzerland and Great Britain have been scouring the area around the picturesque yet terrifying Reichenbach Falls looking for clues. England's ambassador to Switzerland has already visited the ghastly scene.

Not much is yet known, but it seems that two men ascended to the Falls in the Reichenbach Funicular railway, but none came back. It is thought that the men were the celebrated London detective Sherlock Holmes and his companion, a veteran of the Afghan wars, Dr John Watson. Police believe that they were followed by Professor James Moriarty, who has

REICHENBACHFALL-BAHN
FAHRKARTE

042035

PERISHES IN
GGLE AT FALLS

long been an enemy of Mr Holmes, and that he and his henchman, Colonel Sebastian Moran, fought with Holmes and Watson on edge of the thundering cataracts and that one or all of them fell to their dooms. No bodies have yet been discovered and police

The Moriarty One-Man Bathyscaphe

The device performed particularly well, withstanding the pounding pressure of falling water with no ill-effects and moving well in a forward direction (although reverse failed when the rudder was compromised by entangling waterweed).

Visibility not optimum due to foaming water near the surface, but oxygen levels remained high throughout the duration of the operation. Note: consider revising ventilation system to accommodate cigar smoke.

May 20, 1891

Having no memory of my past life is both a little bewildering and somewhat liberating. It seems I had a terrible accident in Meiringen in Switzerland. At least that is where I awoke confused, concussed and barely conscious on the banks of the River Aar. Why I was there in the first place I could not fathom. I have no recollection of reaching the Reichenbach Falls — perhaps I had gone there to view the stunning waterfall and take the air. I enjoyed long strolls in the countryside during my subsequent convalescence from the unexplained event so perhaps that was my motive. All I can clearly recollect is a dreadful headache and being soaked to the bone. I staggered to a nearby house for assistance, a local doctor was summoned and a diagnosis of severe concussion proffered. For my amnesia no explanation or help was forthcoming. He prescribed rest and so I stayed on in Meiringen until fully restored in body, but still suffering strange recurring dreams of falling from the sky, plunging into a vortex of cold water and surfacing in a large, metallic box. I would always awake at that point, exhausted, my head reverberating with pain but exultant at being alive.

June 27, 1891

Now that I am restored, in body if not in memory, I have decided that I must put my future to good use. I can only guess to what purpose I assigned my life before "The Great Fall" but I suspect my desire to benefit others and to do good in the world harks back to life before it. I think a wish to influence the fate of those souls not born with my advantages, to affect their lives, to be an agent of change in an unjust world must have been with me always. I find I recoil from violent behaviour and execrate unkindness in others. This must be an indication of the nature of my beneficient, humanitarian, generous and humble character.

July 7, 1892

I am disconsolate. I struggle still to find identity and purpose in life. A desire to help others burns within.

September 23, 1892

Life in Papua New Guinea suits me remarkably well. A chance meeting with a man in Montpelier set my life on a new course. He told me that he had derived great benefit from travel to distant parts in search of purpose and clarity and put me swiftly in touch with the London Missionary Society. Now I am here, a missionary in Papua New Guinea. I have been so preoccupied that I have not had time to put pen to paper much. Nor have I had any success in retrieving memories of or insights from my past life, although sometimes a fleeting shadow of uncertainty crosses my mind about what life was like before "The Great Fall". And the face of the man in Montpelier haunts me slightly. I have an inkling I knew him in my former life. But this is pure conjecture. The most important thing is that I am doing good with my life.

I arrived in Port Moresby earlier this year and have been travelling ceaselessly from community to community, journeying into the mountains, spreading the teachings as far and wide and as fervidly as I can. What greater, more edifying mission in life could there be? Of course, there is some resistance here but I feel I am making an important contribution. This is what my life was destined to be. I am convinced of it.

September 28, 1894
Felled. A second time. What perfidy! Concussed after surviving another vertiginous descent — now I recall every detail of the event — but in the coconut groves. A sharp and heavy blow and then I came to, recovering my senses, my memory suddenly restored, the dark canvas of my previous life slowly unfurling before my incredulous eyes. The joy at its recollection. The horror of my circumstances. The ignominy of my fall into grace from evil. And H the duplicitous agent of it. I cannot endure nor express it. My doppelgänger horrifies me.

October 14, 1984
Secured a passage on a boat. The listed passenger lost his berth and met his death. I am reborn. I am restored. The life of a missionary was nearly the end, the very downfall of me. I am restored. Moriarty redux!

April 1, 1894

Unbelievable debacle! Did I or did I not instruct Moran most specifically, in monosyllables if I remember, to wait until I was fully returned before tackling Holmes? It is I, Moriarty, who is his nemesis, not old trigger-happy Royal Flush. Look what he does left to his own dunderheaded devices! We had Holmes on the run! He was in a blue funk, creeping around Tibet and Europe in disguise, terrified in case any of my henchmen ever found him. So much for the Great Detective! I was for a little more exquisite torture, a breaking of the spirit, but Moran crashes in like a rogue rhino, shooting his only friend for target practice using a gun that every maiden aunt in the shires knows only he possesses, and setting all Scotland Yard on his heels (they can be bought off but it requires

I knew that Moriarty was not the only man who had sworn my death. There were at least three others whose desire for vengeance upon me would only be increased by the death of their leader. They were all most dangerous men. One or other would certainly get me. On the other hand, if all the world was convinced that I was dead they would take liberties, these men, they would lay themselves open, and sooner or later I could destroy them. Then it would be time for me to announce that I was still in the land of the living. So rapidly does the brain act that I believe I had thought this all out before Professor Moriarty had reached the bottom of the

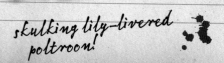

skulking lily-livered poltroon!

146

> "The man that the whole force has been seeking in vain – Colonel Sebastian Moran, who shot the Honourable Ronald Adair with an expanding bullet from an air-gun through the open window of the second-floor front of No. 427, Park Lane, upon the 30th of last month. That's the charge, Lestrade. And now, Watson, if you can endure the draught from a broken window, I think that half an hour in my study over a cigar may afford you some profitable amusement."

Insufferable condescending prig!

a finesse that Moran does not dream of). I improvised a disguise of dark spectacles and tried to derail Watson in Park Lane, but it was too late. And as for Parker as lookout, the man who insists on playing the Jew's harp on every job and is therefore the most recognisable thug in town. Holmes may flatter Moran as the second most dangerous man in London (to make himself look more impressive, of course), but as far as I am concerned he is the second most boneheaded. I am minded not to spring the unadulterated halfwit from this one.

And do you know the most galling thing about this utter shambles? It's having to read Doyle's extravagantly boot-licking account of it all with Watson fawning about like a great galumphing girl – what a broken reed he has proved to be.

Ungrateful swine!!!!!!!!!!!!!

★ ★ ★

MISSION: to flex my international muscles and to win Elsie Patrick for myself. From Illinois to Norfolk, from crook-crammed Chicago to tree-lined country manors in England, my network can fell a man and take a woman. He may lay claim to the dark streets or to a family reputation of five generations, but I shall have his soul or his head and his woman

Patrick was the boss of the Joint in Chicago until I relieved him of the burden of the role. A cunning, cruel criminal, he reminded me of myself but painted in paler hues. We did some excellent business together and recruited minions to do the worst of it. Abe Slaney took crime by the neck like a mongoose does an adder, enjoying the fight, the victory and the blood. I did my best to keep his mind on crime but he fell for Patrick's daughter, Elsie, whose father promised her as his prize. The girl, soft hearted and blindly virtuous, turned her back on the gang and fled the attentions of Slaney by heading to London. I was happy to help him track her down after she married Hilton Cubitt, manor owner in Norfolk, soon after — at a price of my naming but it was a mere ruse to disguise my own intentions. Did she feel safer in the arms of that Establishment than our own? We both take what we feel we have a right to. We both wield power over others and use force to procure and defend our own. We are different sides of the same coin. Light and shade exchange reflections in a mirror.

And we know how to make them!

Slaney doted on Elsie but was not her match. My plan
was for him to release her from Cubitt and then take
her for myself. The lovelorn, hot-headed fool used
the code I taught the gang to communicate with the
now married Elsie. I knew it would not be long before
Cubitt sought help in the matter when notes were left
on the sundial and door and it would only be a question
of time before the eminent breaker of codes, solver
of riddles and author of a book upon the subject was
called in. I encouraged Slaney all the while to play
his hand, goading him to temper, forcing his hand
while Sherlock studied the hieroglyphic fruits of
it. I knew that it would lead to a climax of violence
for Cubitt and, I hoped, Slaney, leaving me free
to rescue Elsie from the ashes of her marriage and
wrong decision. And — sweet victory — Holmes got
there too late, he should stick to writing about codes
— pah! Of course he decoded the facts and Slaney was
arrested. None of which perturbed me.

NOTES: But I did not bank upon Elsie being so badly
injured by her own hand or that once recovered she
would continue in her path of virtue. What do I know
of women? I shall undertake a thorough scientific
investigation to expose the female psyche.

* * *

MISSION: to test H's mettle, to challenge his much
praised powers; to ease the boredom that pervades
my soul; to keep active a mind, which with the lack
of crime to occupy it could become weak and prone
to feeble thoughts of virtue

Bored, gripped by lassitude, stagnating in a vacuum.
No evil plan simmering in the homicidal corner of
my brain. I craved an injection of criminal intent.
No seven percent solution for me. I wanted a barrel
of it. I devised a fiendish puzzle, a bloody game,
for Holmes and Watson, the eminent detective and
sycophantic doctor, lured by Lestrade. I needed a
sacrificial bait and found one with ease. Time spent
in the drinking dens among sailors soon bore fruit,
for if there is a concentration of disillusion, vice
and crime anywhere it is there. I soon had a man in
my thrall whose blood coursed with vengeful fury,
tormented by his faithless wife and the machinations
of her jealous sister. I poured poison into his ears,
each drop matched by a slug from the rum bottle he
had once foresworn. Jim Browner had lost his wife
Mary to a charmer Fairbairn and his wits to drink
but both losses he blamed on his sister-in-law Sarah,
whose unsisterly advances he had rejected at his
peril. His hatred of both was easily fortified with
rum words and lubrication as plied by me — and what
enjoyment it brought me in my hiatus of crime! Soon
Jim Browner's mind was flailing in a Niagara-like

torrent of murderous revenge and he followed his wife
and her lover to New Brighton and killed them in a
rowing boat, slicing an ear from each. With ease
and satisfaction I persuaded the sailor to post the
bloodied severed trophies in salt in a parcel with
knotted string to his sister-in-law for I knew it
would soon bring Lestrade to the bait and Holmes to
my trawling net, the great author of monographs on
the variations of this fascinating body part. No
matter that he did not know where the hated Sarah
lived now. She had eluded me too. It just added to
the intrigue. But Holmes was more interested in his
violin than in my bloody japer. Boasting about the
ease of it. Not wanting his name involved. Snubbing
his nose at me. He will regret it.

NOTES: I shall have to widen, deepen, reinforce my
circle of misery, violence and fear. I shall devise
a crime that H cannot resist, but cannot solve; a
heinous happening that brings me satisfaction and
him frustration.

JORAM MAYSHIRE

PURVEYORS OF

EXCELSIOR

COARSE PACKING SALT
ESTABLISHED 1888

by appointment

ROTHERHITHE, LIVERPOOL & NOVOSIBIRSK

221b — hazards and vulnerabilities

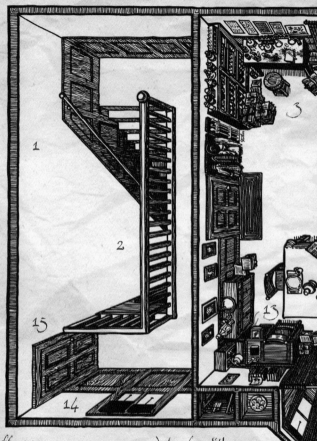

1) defensible staircase
2) easily loosened handrail
3) fire hazard (chemicals)
4) unoverlooked window
5) heavy curtains to hide behind
6) stairs to Watson's room

7) door from SH room to backstairs
8) basket to hide in
9) window vulnerable from Baker Street
10) passage between SH room and bay window area

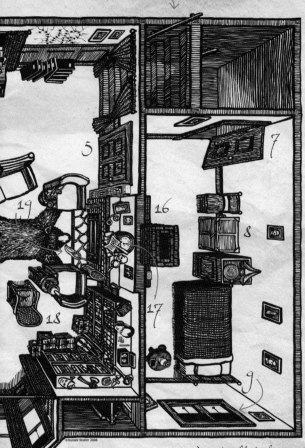

6 ↓

5

7

19

16

8

18

17

9

10

11) three-way vulnerability
 through bay window

12) screen to hide bodies

13) Watson's service revolver

14) window blinds for signalling

15) Mrs Hudson's room

16) chimney for ingress and blocking

17) jack-knife if in need of weapon

18) fire hazard (paper)

19) tobacco (easily poisoned)

©Russell Stutler 2008

* * *

MISSION: to extract Mycroft Holmes and Her Majesty's Government from a politically sensitive and embarrassing debacle re: the Bruce-Partington Project

Mycroft Holmes came to me at the Diogenes Club as exercised as I have ever seen him; he had intelligence that the Bruce-Partington Project, an elaborate hoax to make other nations think Britain had an ultimate deterrent, was about to be exposed by Sir John Walter, the deluded fool who thought he was in charge of an actual weapon. Fortuitously, his brother Captain Valentine Walter was an indifferent gambler, and Moran soon had him so far in hock he was ripe for blackmail. If it had not been for the interfering hero Cadogan West, the handover to our agent Oberstein (in England on another mission) and the destruction of the papers would have gone smoothly. Oberstein, thoughtless psychopath, killed West, planted some of the papers on him and threw him onto a train roof and the operation open to the public.

Against my counsel, Mycroft involved his little brother unknowingly to generate a smoke screen of self-important busyness to distract the eye from the truth. Colonel Walter was thrown to the wolves (serves him right) and I allowed Oberstein to be sacrificed, as his ungovernable violence cost the organisation dear. These government contracts offer prestige but no concomitant emolument.

NOTES: Another chance to test moriartium in the field; not even Mycroft suspects that Sir James Walter died of anything other than mortification.

UNDERGROUND ELECTRIC RAILWAYS OF LONDON

Photo # NH 77191   General plan of submarine Holland, 1899

HORIZONTAL SECTION.

PLAN OF SUPERSTRUCTURE.

LONGITUDINAL SECTION.

MISSION: to take down Sir Eustace Brackenstall.
To reduce his circumstances and take him down,
so low he is below ground

My hatred for Brackenstall, bullying drunkard from
the undeserving landed gentry, took root when he
tried to dupe the innocent Marjory Samite. She
escaped his clutches but the scar remained and
became my own. I played the long game, waiting for
an opportunity to take him. Brackenstall lured
a young Australian woman, Miss Mary Fraser of
Adelaide, with the promise of money and title,
and she trod the same path as Marjory but past the
altar. Word of her suffering reached me from Abbey
Grange, where I had staff in my pay, and of a close
acquaintance with Captain Croker during her journey
to England aboard one of the ships in my fleet —
Rock of Gibraltar. Croker was a man of naïve but
useful virtue, with a calm head at sea and a temper
on land, so I arranged for his next vessel, **Bass Rock**,
to be delayed by two months at Southampton and
counted upon him trying to see Miss Fraser, now the
miserable Lady Brackenstall, living not far from his
home. I waited for Fate to play its hand at cards, my
own ready with their royal flush, which now included
the canny old maid Theresa. Croker duly visited Mary
and, strong and fiery as I had predicted, avenging
her, dispatched Brackenstall with the poker.
Theresa concocted a cover with three wine glasses,
a burglary and knotted bell rope that had notorious
Randalls written all over it, curs and duffers that

have to date eluded my grasp. The plot could have
foiled and blinded the police had H not intervened,
summoned by hapless Hopkins. But the mission was
not botched by H. I was not tied up by him, despite
his infernal knowledge of knots, and — delicious,
deadly irony — a man of blind virtue executed my
own dark plan. Holmes, always considering himself
above the law, better than it, and arbiter of it,
released Croker, and I can still use Theresa.

NOTES: Keep cool head while all about lose theirs.
This was Holmes's Marengo. The game's afoot?
I think not!

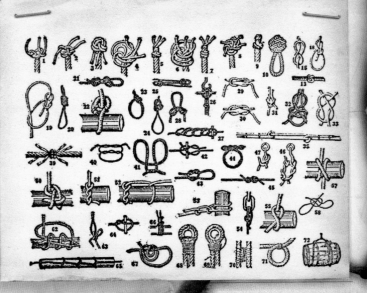

***

MISSION: to frighten a foe and wrong-doer out of his wits or life

And me

Nobody wrongs my circle and lives long to tell the tale. If a man insults me in the springtime of his years, he will not live to see the summer of them. Many a foe has taken an early and uncomfortable journey to eternity using a ticket issued by me. And so it was with Colonel Barclay, as unpleasant a high-ranking, low-dealing blaggard as you could hope to encounter. Barclay had recently snubbed Moran at a club. The Colonel, not a man to take such an insult until the other fellow was face down in the mud, had known Sergeant Barclay — as was his rank then — when they were both in India. Their different routes in life, both pitted with violence, had crossed on occasion, and Moran had sworn more than once that he might prove useful as air-rifle target practice. Time and fate played into our hands when we met an old soldier, Henry Wood, broken by Barclay; a corporal delivered to the enemy at the time of the Indian mutiny by the vindictive sergeant, jealous of his rival for the affections of Nancy, his future wife. Broken in spirit and spine, Wood performed tricks for money for soldiers with a snake-catching mongoose, which I offered to buy in order to trick and torment, but he refused. Even when largely vicarious, the sweet taste of revenge satisfies. We urged the man without means or rancour to challenge his nemesis. He traced Nancy, informed her of his fate, and the

mere sight of him killed Barclay, the latter's
conscience dispatching him more swiftly than any
bullet could.

NOTES: Of course Holmes was soon upon the trail and
tail, solving the riddle of the mongoose and the
dead Colonel, but he was just a bit player. I was the
director of events. A victory for me. The sweetness
is with me still.

May 5, 1895

My natural inclination will always be to crime. Its widespread organisation and effects remain my principal preoccupation. My career — and my campaign against Holmes — will always be at the forefront of my meticulous and superior mind, but I would not be a rounded character if I did not have interests outside these. My heart is not in such full employ as my brain, but it is an important organ all the same and, as is commonly known, a man of great intelligence and influence will always attract the attentions both of his own and the opposite sex. Napoleon had his Josephine, his Pauline, his Marie, his Marie-Louise, his Helene, his Desiree, and so I am not surprised to find myself the recent object of the affections of at least two very different, but beautiful and talented, women:

Marjory Samite

love is blind-folded!

Marjory Jamite, an English rose and niece of one of my business contacts, is as sweet as she is sagacious, as flattering as she is fresh and floral, as intelligent and quick-witted as she is devoted and affectionate. I spend many intimate hours with her, advising her and sharing with her my knowledge of this world, guiding

Joy Aimer Smart

her through life's maze. I fear she is besotted with me and that a decision may be required soon. I am also very drawn to an American heiress, Joy Aimer Smart, a spirited woman from New York who enjoys the darker aspect of my nature and who is as beautiful as she is beguiling, as mysterious as she is mischievous, as devoted as she is distracting. Irene is insanely jealous of both women but too proud to show it.

***

MISSION: to eliminate a defective, defecting
operative and recruit fresh, bad blood

My international distribution network was providing
me with a handsome income, when I heard that one of
my regulars wanted to exchange a life of lucrative
export and import for one of Sussex domesticity with
a new wife and baby! Ferguson had been my man in
nitrates in Peru and had perfected an excellent
front as a tea merchant, a cover it was vital to
protect. He wanted to defect, make up for his past
life. The ravings of a mind softened by sentiment.

Irene made an excellent nurse for the new child,
convincing in her disguise, and was willing to execute
the Peruvian plan: to harm the baby and lay blame at
the new wife's door. Preliminary dart tests went well
on the dog but Jacky, Ferguson's disabled, envious
fifteen year-old with a burgeoning criminal mind, got
wind of it and tried the same on the child. No option
but to call in a favour at Morrison, Morrison and Dodd
— how easy it was given the incident last year — and
persuade the deluded Ferguson, thinking his wife a
vampire, to implore Holmes to help, promising to release
him if he did so. I couldn't risk any police not in my
pay exposing us.

NOTES: Wrong-footed but enjoyed watching H in his
resolution of the supernatural. Master Jacky became
mine after being sent to sea for his part in it.
He will make a good minion for marine missions...

Dear Arthur

Bound as we are by a distant blood tie and, I had hoped, the close kinship of fellow authors, I feel compelled to express my feelings about the tale in which you cast vampires in an unjustifiably poor light. "Flatfooted upon the ground" as your esteemed and capable detective, Sherlock Holmes, has every right to be, I expected more of your good self. My concern is not that you are writing about a subject similar to my own, although in a much abbreviated form, but that you do not show the appropriate respect for it.

Yours sincerely,

Bram Stoker

Intercepted by a postman in my pay!

Desmodus rotundus
(native to Sussex)

Where the deuce is Moriarty? Vanished, gone, no word of where and, here's the worst, no note or notes for me. Abandoned by the Professor, left to live upon me wits on London's streets. Chief-of-staff without remit, recompense or remedy. The snake. Should have smelled a rat, though; after Holmes ambushed me in Baker Street, Moriarty left me to rot in the cells for three whole days before he deigned to spring me, and that bally peeler Lestrade wouldn't even get a feller a decent drink. Ungrateful swine. What reward for me loyal work, for carryin' out his most perilous commands, for the faithful execution of his orders and enemies? Didn't relish shootin' Mrs Stewart, but did I default on duty?

Sold what I could after the fire. As I said, I was out of the country at the time. Persuaded Morris, Meatjay to publish these papers (they did me own books) for a paltry figure, but apparently I didn't earn out my advance, and now I find they've levanted. Have to lay low as any influence I had in Scotland Yard has faded away just like the Professor. Perilously near to hocking me gun; needs must when tin runs low, and there ain't too many tigers in London.

No Moran, it's back to the wars for you; a man can get lost in the fog of war don't you know, and I always feel comfortable in conflict; the soldier's life's a simple one if he don't weaken.

Col. Sebastian Moran

PS People still askin' me who the blighter really is. I have no idea. Why should I care as long as the money rolled in? If I knew, I would sell to the highest bidder now faster than a bullet from my trusty companion takes to sever an artery, but I don't. He was an odd cove though — fierce brain, always plotting — not my sort at all. Put me in mind of Sherlock Holmes sometimes, but would never have told him so. Was worth more than my life to.

Afterword

WE DISCOVERED THIS NOTE BY COLONEL MORAN folded in the back of the single remaining copy of the original book found in Morris, Meatjay's old offices and decided to include it in our facsimile for historical interest, and for his cryptic remarks about the whereabouts and identity of Professor Moriarty. We know it is in Moran's hand, as it corresponds with the foreword and his illuminating marginal comments found in the original, and reproduced in the facsimile. It bears no date.

SOLUTIONS TO CIPHERS ON PAGE 62 & 63

***

PIGPENS

The classic pigpen cipher is based on the pigpen grid

A	B	C
D	E	F
G	H	I

J	K	L
M	N	O
P	Q	R

To create the pigpen code, substitute every letter with the shape the lines make around it including the dots — the 'pen' rather than the 'pig' in it. So, for example, A is ⌐.

PIGPEN SOLUTIONS: i) RAMSEY JAM RIOT ii) JEMMY SARTORIA iii) CAPE ME SI POTES iv) MORIARTY v) MORITURI vi) MORAN vii) QUOD NOMEN MIHI EST viii) MEMENTO MORI ARTE MORTUA ix) ARS MORIENDI x) NAPOLEON OF CRIME xi) MAY MORIARTIUM BE MY ART OF DEATH

SHIFTED PIGPEN

This works like a pigpen, but uses a key word, in this case MORAN, for the first five letters then runs the rest of the alphabet, excluding those letters, as a standard pigpen.

SHIFTED PIGPEN SOLUTION: Irene Adler

ELDER FUTHARK

This uses the elder futhark, a runic alphabet, to transcribe words.

F U Th A R K G W H N I J æ P Z S T B E M L ng O D

ELDER FUTHARK SOLUTION: Moriartium

DANCING MEN

Readers are referred to The Adventure of the Dancing Men by A.C. Doyle for instructions on how to crack this code

DANCING MEN SOLUTION: Charles Milverton